From Russia With Fur

rene fomby

Book Ness
Monster
Press

Book Ness Monster Press
4530 Blue Ridge Drive
Belton, Texas 76513

Visit us on the World Wide Web: http://www.renefomby.com

Fomby, Rene. From Russia With Fur.
Book Ness Monster Press.
Paperback Edition.

To Moose and Fat Tony

Heaven may never be the same

Downtown Chicago,
One Month Earlier

I n quieter times, he'd have headed home hours earlier, and already been curled up next to the fire, trying to exorcise the bone chilling cold of the last few months out of his system. Exorcise the demons that had been haunting him for all those months, demons that laughed at him from the pages of almost every report that had crossed his desk lately.

He shivered in the damp, dark cold of the alleyway as he set the alarm to the office and pulled the door closed, locking it carefully and double-checking to make sure everything was secure. Even on an ordinary day you just couldn't afford to leave things to chance, to leave any stone unturned. And these days were anything but ordinary.

Sure, the morning had started off on a good note. Breakfast as usual, gone in a gulp or three, barely tasted. His morning constitutional, a walk down the Miracle Mile. And things had finally seemed to be settling down a bit lately, the whole prison break thing at Southside becoming old news, the hunt for all the escapees slowly fading into history.

But then the pee-mail had popped up. From M in London, of all people. And the startling news that sent a frozen tendril trickling down his furry spine. The Russians were coming.

A noise from close behind startled him, and he quickly ducked down and checked over his left shoulder to see who—or what—it was. But then a cane materialized out of the fog-shrouded alley, a cane with a razor sharp tip that plunged immediately into his upper haunches. And then everything went black.

Hyde Park,
Early Sunday Morning

I'd have to call these the dog days of winter. I mean, I don't really understand why humans call the hottest, sultriest days in the middle of August the dog days of summer—that's an insult to the canine race—but if ever there was a day meant for a dog, this would be it. The wet, gray blanket that had hung over Chicago almost every day for the past few months was finally headed home, hopefully for good, and even though it was still a bit on the brisk side outdoors, the sun had somehow managed to force its way through the clouds and was blissfully lighting up my backyard like those tiny little heaters my humans still had scattered all throughout the house.

I carefully poked my nose once, then twice at the new door. My master spent several hours installing it yesterday afternoon, and just this morning he attached a little thingamajig to my collar that was supposed to make it all work, make it unlock the door whenever I needed to head outside. But you know, you can never be too careful with these things. I mean, even with my old low-tech doggie door, I had more than a few unfortunate face-to-face encounters with a swinging door that simply refused to swing when it needed to. I'm talking head trauma that woulda make a hockey star wince.

But I gotta appreciate this whole computerized doggie door thing. Especially after everything I went through just the other day, framed for the full-scale destruction of our kitchen I had absolutely nothing to do with. Well, okay, I wasn't exactly on full-scale sentry duty that night, but hey, every soldier gets a free pass out on the town every now and then, am I right? And it's not like I had any advance warning of the assault. So I think it's fair to say my humans went more than a little over the top in how they reacted. Just sayin'.

Okay, yeah, a few dishes got dented up a bit here and there. Not much different than my own water bowl, and you don't hear me complaining, right? And, yeah, the pull-out drawer on the freezer got pulled out all night long. That could have been anyone's mistake, and it's not like I was in any way interested in frozen peas and chunks of meat that could just as well have come from the Alaskan tundra. After several years of being abandoned in the bottom of the drawer, those bags could have been chunks of mastodon meat for all I knew. Or cared. My humans really need to sit down and come up with some kind of inventory system for all that, some way of keeping track of what they've stashed away for leaner days in the future, when the handouts don't hand out all that well. I mean, you think I don't know where I've hidden my own personal cache of half-eaten bones and chewsticks? Got it down to a science, I promise you. A science.

Okay, where was I? Oh, yeah! The doggie door. The thing is, for about a day or so I was really in the doghouse around here. Well, not a real doghouse. This is Chicago, after all, and for most of the year an outside shelter isn't really all that practical, no matter how well it's insulated. In fact, that's the sort of thing PETSEC was meant to address in the first place, humans mistreating the very animals God created humans to protect in the first place. So, when I say doghouse, I only mean it in the metaphorical way. I was in a whole lot of trouble. Like I might miss a din-din kind of trouble.

That's where Bella fits into the story. I mean, you gotta understand, I love Bella. She's my very best friend, especially since Killer left town, but—she's a talker, you know what I mean? Always has something to say, even when nobody's listening. And that's especially problematical for us dogs, because God gave us big noses and big ears for a reason, if you catch my drift. Humans have this thing about pretending they can't hear when their girlfriends start up about this and that, but we dogs got no excuse. Well, no excuse when it comes to other dogs. With humans we play deaf all the time.

Okay, I kinda got off track there. Something about Bella. And the doggie door. Oh yeah! So I'm in serious trouble with my humans, and they've kangaroo courted me on the whole kitchen thing—by the way, if you've ever met a kangaroo, they punch first and ask questions later, so the court thing makes a lot of sense—when what do you know, Bella corners a full-on bandit of a raccoon in her own kitchen, dead to rights! Sets off an alarm that probably triggered earthquake alerts across the entire state! I don't know if you've ever experienced a Corgi in full bark mode, but it's a sonic weapon that could wake the dead. Or at least make you wish you were dead. A true force of nature that seems anything but natural.

So Bella's humans at some point managed to pull themselves away from Rachel Ray long enough to check out what Bella had been going on and on about, and they found this raccoon cowering in the corner of the kitchen, completely cowed by Bella's overpowering sonic blasts. (A feeling I can sympathize with, having been on the business end of her toxic tongue myself.)

Bottom line is, raccoon got reassigned to a new neighborhood, Bella got a gold star, and I got human food as a make-up din-din. Not a bad resolution to the problem, all in all.

And that brings me back to the new doggie door. As it turns out, raccoons don't wear collars, so they can't wear the little thingamajigs that open the computerized doggie doors. Problem solved! Yeah, I had to learn a little restraint, not go blasting through the door full-tilt at every provocation, but at my age that's probably a good thing. Take things one moment at a time, like when I get fed human food. Not one quick gulp, mind you, but instead take the time to sit back and enjoy it. Three gulps, at least. Okay, two, but who's counting, anyway? For sure, not any dog near me!

Back to the doggie door. After a few test nudges, my collar seems to be working out just fine, so I head straight outside for some long-overdue nap time out in the warm morning sun. A quick glance in Bella's direction tells me she's not outside yet, and then I remember. She had to go to the hospital this morning to get her nose patched up where the raccoon got in a lucky swipe. And she seemed pretty upset about all that, worried about having a big scar on her face the rest of her life, literally front and center. But that's okay by me. It's the little imperfections that really bring out the beauty in a woman, don't you think?

Anyway, the sun has already warmed up a nice dog-sized stretch of grass right next to my oak tree— the leaves aren't out yet, so shade is still a month or so away, but I'll take the sun right now any day of the week. I circle the sunny spot a few times, just to make sure everything's perfect, then ease into a nice tight ball. I'm asleep almost before I hit the ground, my paws already starting to twitch in anticipation.

POW! What the— POW POW! The sudden frontal assault seemed to come out of nowhere. I try to get to my feet, but my legs still seem a little wobbly,

8

and I've got way too much sleepy in my eyes to see straight right about now. POW! POW POW POW!

I manage to drag a paw across my eyes, and then—there! I see him! A giant squirrel! Perched on top of the fence between my yard and Bella's! And it's hurling acorns at me with the force of a submachine gun!

"What the heck?" I sputter. Quickly I dodge behind the trunk of the oak tree, catching one last stinging shot across my haunches as I race for cover. It's my old nemesis, Sammy Squirrel! Oh, he's going to pay for this one big time. This time he's gone too far. I had been just inches from latching onto that bicycle tire. Inches! You don't come across dreams like that every day, and now it's all ruined. Lost in the wind forever.

"Squirrel, what the heck do you think you're doing?"

Sammy is smirking at me from on top of the fence. "Good to see you up and about, Moose. Took you long enough. I went through almost half of my stash of ammo trying to wake you up. And acorns like that don't exactly grow on trees, you know."

I am just about to explain to him that, yeah, duh, acorns do grow on trees—on the very same oak tree I was hiding behind, as a matter of fact—when I realize just how stupid that would be. I mean, you can't have a reasonable conversation with a squirrel, it's just not done. Tree rats got brains the size of my front dew claws. Part of what makes them all so annoying, cluttering up my backyard, chittering away at nothing all the time.

"Okay, Squirrel, I'll give you ten seconds to come up with some good explanation for your behavior, then I'll—"

"Then you'll do what, Yorkie? Climb this fence and come after me? With those tiny little legs of yours? That I gotta see!"

Yorkie! Why, that little… It only takes one good long look to see I'm no Yorkie. I'm a full-bred Australian Terrier. AKC registered, for that matter. Well, not exactly, to be totally honest. Seems the paperwork for that must've got lost in the mail. Right after the parts that marked me as a male got lost, as well. But no question about it, I'm one hundred percent Aussie, tough as they come. Ten pounds of lean, mean fighting machine. I managed to take out that Doberman that attacked Bella virtually single-handedly, didn't I? If my mistress hadn't butted in like she did and swatted him down the street with her broom, that dog would've have been mincemeat, no question about it.

But again, we're back to the futility of having an adult conversation with a pea-brained squirrel, so I gotta just let it go.

"You'll get yours someday, Squirrel, I promise you that. But, back to the subject, why did you think it might be a good idea to bean me with a pile of acorns, especially given it's the first nice day we've had around here in months?"

Sammy chitters something under his breath I don't quite catch, then sets the two acorns he was holding in his paws down on the top rail of the fence and turns toward me with a serious look. "To be honest, Moose, the less time I spend around a bark-brain like you the better. But I got instructions from the top. You're wanted downtown, like on the double. There's some secret meeting going on down at headquarters."

"Headquarters? Downtown? What the heck are you chittering on about?" Even on a good day, squirrels never make much sense, and this one is losing me completely. What business could I possibly have downtown? I mean, I'm a suburban pooch, I don't know a soul out in that godforsaken neck of the woods. Well, not a soul except—

Sammy cocks his small head sarcastically. "PETSEC, you lap dog idiot! Who else do you think would have a headquarters in downtown Chicago? The stock market? McDonalds? Sheesh!"

PETSEC? Boy, I hadn't heard that name since the whole Killer thing, since we broke my best buddy out of his death row cell down at Southside Prison and got him settled into a new home. Which reminds me, I am way overdue paying him a visit and catching up…

The squirrel tosses another acorn in my direction, rather haphazardly this time, and it bounces harmlessly off the grass in front of my feet. "Did you hear me, furball?" he shouts. "Headquarters wants your brown overstuffed butt downtown like yesterday, so you better get a move on. And with those tiny little legs of yours, it'll probably take you a month to get there, anyways, if you even make it at all."

I look down at the acorn, then back up at the squirrel. PETSEC or not, this guy still had some 'splaining to do. "What in the world would PETSEC want with me? And how in the world are you connected with them? That's a pet protection organization, after all. No squirrels allowed."

Sammy spat on the ground in front of the fence. "Believe it or not, Yorkie, we squirrels are an integral part of the organization. We make up the very core of PETSEC's perimeter alert system. The Distant Early Warning Squirrels, they call us. DEWS, for short."

"But you can't be part of PETSEC, for gosh sakes! You're not pets," I splutter, completely confused by now. Squirrels? In PETSEC? It'll never happen.

The squirrel's lips pull back threateningly, baring all his teeth. Gotta say, never seen a tree rat do that before now. "Who says we're not pets, Mooselet? We're just outside pets, is all, like a lot of cats. Why, the humans have been putting out nice little squirrel feeders since the dawn of time, filled to the top with delicious morsels of seed, just in case we ever run short of nuts. Sometimes they even put little covers on them, to keep the raccoons out. And, truth be told, we probably need PETSEC's protection even more than you purse doggies do."

That's preposterous, and I make no bones telling him so. "Yeah? And why is that, exactly? You guys got it made. Free food, free housing up in the trees. No natural predators." I have to pause for a second on that one. But, to be fair, I've never actually caught a squirrel before. Don't really know what I'd do with one if I did. I mean, what self-respecting dog would ever want one of those mangy flea-bitten things in its mouth? Just the thought of it would put me off kibble for a month, I tell you. But, back to the conversation. Squirrels have a way of distracting me.

A haunted look crosses Sammy's face for just a fleet second. "You got no idea, Moose. You got no idea what we squirrels go through on a day-to-day basis. I mean, you ever been shot at by a human in your own back yard? They even hand out pellet guns to their little humans and send them outside to hunt us down. And just for the fun of it, mind you. They kill us just for the fun of it. I mean, I can understand it if they're all starving to death and hunting for food, like they did back in the day. That's just the circle of life, after all, and you can't blame someone for trying to feed their family. But—"

A tear starts trickling down Sammy's gray cheek, and suddenly I feel like a complete heel for ever bringing the subject up in the first place. He wipes the tear away slowly with his left paw and looks straight at me. "I was there, you know. I was just a little squirrel at the time, just barely out of the nest, but I was there. When the human kid across the alley shot my mom. In cold blood, and then left her there to bleed out. Left her there to die." He suddenly stops talking as he starts breathing funny and covers both of his eyes with one paw.

I don't know what to say. I'm never all that good at moments like these, so I decide the best idea is just to change the subject. "So, hey, Sammy, you said I'm wanted at HQ. Where exactly is that? I mean, my dealings with those folks have always been a little paws-off, arm's length transactions, if you know what I mean. I've never even voted in one of their elections, to be honest. So where are we supposed to meet up?"

Sammy takes a long moment to recover, then finally drops his paw. I can't help but notice his eyes looking bright red. Raw. He's not looking in my direction when he answers. "I was told they were all meeting up at Fat Tony's office. That you would know how to find it."

Fat Tony? Why, I haven't thought about him for one moment, not since our last meet-up in his office. And for good reason. "Hold on, Sammy. I—I don't get it. I've been to Tony's office a bunch of times, and I never saw anything that looked like a pet protection operation going on in there. Did I miss something?"

"Didn't you hear?" Sammy asks, finally looking my way. "Fat Tony's been named interim president of PETSEC, ever since the previous president was found lying dead just outside his office about a month ago. The elections to name a new, permanent president are set for Tuesday, and Fat Tony is expected to win it by a landslide. And that'll truly be something, a first time for everything. Never had a cat at the top of PETSEC, before. As a matter of fact, none of them ever seemed to be all that interested in the job."

Now I'm feeling like a complete idiot. Here I am, a dog, and this—squirrel—knows more about PETSEC than I could ever imagine. Maybe Bella is right about me. Maybe I do live too sheltered a life, lounging around out here in the 'burbs. Maybe I do need to get more involved in things. But then I think about the last time I got involved in business outside of our safe little neighborhood, and I think, nah! I can't count how many times I almost got myself killed in just two short days, poking my nose into things best left alone. But at least I'd managed to save my buddy Killer. And freed a bunch of other wrongly-imprisoned dogs and cats in the process.

I sneak a peek over at the spot under the old mulberry bush where there's a hole leading out into the alley. If I'm going to make the meeting, I better get going. Fat Tony will have my hide if I show up fashionably late, for sure. But as I start to head that way, one final thing stops me in my tracks.

"Okay, listen up Sammy, I'll let things slide between you and me for now. But tell me, did you really have to whack me like that with the acorns? You couldn't have just nudged me a little, all gentle like, so I could have eased out of my dreams instead of being jolted awake?" I feel the left side of my head, where I swear a huge knot is already starting to swell up.

Sammy laughs out loud, a funny sound coming from a squirrel, kind of like claws scraping across a sidewalk. "Nudge you? That's hilarious, Moose! You should do standup, for sure!" He takes a second to get control of himself, then goes on. "You ever hear the phrase, let sleeping dogs lie? You think for a second I'd have risked being just inches away from those canines of yours when you woke up? Not in a million years, I tell you! Not in a million years!"

The squirrel has a point. After all, we have some history between us, Sammy and me. Sure, for me it was all mostly just fun and games, but then—I've never seen my mom shot down right in front of me. In cold blood. That sort of thing has got to change a guy, for sure, and not in a good way. As I trot over to the mulberry bush to make my way downtown to the meeting, the thought crosses my mind that maybe I could mend fences a little with the squirrel, after all. Cut him a little slack, maybe even be friends.

But that thought only lasts a second. Maybe two at the most. I mean, he is a squirrel, after all…

Downtown Chicago, Mid-Morning

I t's been more than a little while since my last trip downtown—ever since the Killer caper, to be exact—and it took me a little longer than I thought to work out all the details with the whole elevated train business. But I made it here in one piece and didn't get myself arrested by some do-gooder for riding without a master, so I'm feeling pretty good about myself as I stroll up to Fat Tony's office, dodging the humans along the way.

As I push the door open with my nose, I can see that very little has changed. The office is still decorated in old leather and dark wood paneling, and dominated by a large oak desk parked right in front of a big picture window looking out over the Chicago skyline. There are so many certificates and awards and photos covering the walls, they might as well have been wallpaper. But I make note of the fact that all of the pictures are of humans grinning at each other, and none of the awards say anything at all about Fat Tony.

Speaking of which, as I trot into the room, Tony is standing right in front of the window, staring out, a fat stogie giving up its last stinking moments of life in an ashtray on the left side of the desk. There are two high-backed chairs laid out in front of me, and as I clear my throat to get Tony's attention, a familiar black-and-white face pokes out from behind the seat off to my right. Tommy Tuxedo. The ultimate fat cat.

"I told you he couldn't be trusted with a mission this big, this important," Tommy snarls in my direction. "Can't even show up on time for the meeting."

Fat Tony turns slowly away from the window, pausing for just a second to give Tommy the stink eye, then glancing my way with a warm smile.

"Moose! It's been too long, my friend."

I smile back, carefully ignoring the harsh look I'm getting from the Tuxedo. "Yeah, it's hard to imagine it's been almost a year already." I point my nose at his gut. "But hey, you've slimmed down quite a bit since the prison break thing. I'm impressed. May have to try out a new nickname, for a change, to go with the new body. Maybe, say, Not-So-Fat Tony? Or how about Antonio Slim?"

Tony pats his belly a couple of times, and for once it doesn't look like it has a life of its own. "I wish

I could say I've been working out to get rid of the weight, but the truth is, this past year has been a hard one. I've missed a lot of meals lately, you know, from all the stress."

"The dress? You mean... you've been..." I direct my eyes a little lower.

"No," Tommy butts in with a sour look on his face. "He said 'stress,' you idiot, not 'dress.' Stress from everything that's been going on around here. Especially since the murder."

Murder? I can barely believe what I'm hearing. There hasn't been a murder in Chicago since Penny got mauled by the Crimson Canines. Well, not among pets, that is. The humans are knocking each other off all the time. I glance over at Tony, who's nodding.

"Moose, you better take a seat. We've got a lot to catch up on, I'm afraid."

I circle around to the front of the empty chair off to my left and hop on up. Which takes more effort than you might think. I mean, I may have the ripped physique of a trained mastiff, but still, with these short legs ...

Tony hops up on the desk himself, facing us. Even slimmed down he's a big cat, a Maine Coon Cat to be exact, with thick gray and brown hair marked with streaks of black, and ears poking up out of all that fur like two little gray horns. Devil's horns, Bella used to call them. Personally, I think they're kind of cute, in a cat-like sort of way.

Tony clears his throat to get our attention. Or maybe he's just working on a big hairball—it's kinda hard to tell with cats.

"Okay, Moose, I gotta warn you, what I'm about to disclose to you is top secret information. Eyes only, and not to be discussed outside of this room. *Capisce*?"

There he goes with that fake Italian accent again. I'm about to say something when I glance over at Tommy and see that he's clearly still bought into the act. Maybe he doesn't know that Tony is actually Jewish, that he's been pulling the wool over everyone's eyes all this time, just pretending to be Italian. Everyone but me, that is. W-e-l-l, to be honest, it was Bella who first tipped me off to the whole phony cannelloni thing. But hey, I was at least the second one to catch on! That's gotta count for something!

But it only takes one quick glance in Tommy's direction to decide this might not be the best time to bring it up. Maybe later. I turn my attention back to Tony, who's talking.

"So here's the deal, Moose. A couple of months after I saw you last, I got a late-night summons from the top brass at PETSEC. Seems the president was concerned that someone might be hacking into his pee-mails, planning something nefarious. Only he couldn't figure out who was doing the hacking, or what they were ultimately up to."

"Pee-mails? You mean hikies? Sniffing around the old fire hydrant?" I'm confused. Sure, you could find out a lot about whoever had been hanging around an area by checking out what he'd left behind, but that was pretty much limited to name, rank and cereal number. Nothing that could really be of much use…

"I can see you're confused, Moose," Tony suggests. "You're probably thinking, how much info could someone get off a random sniff of a tree trunk, and normally you'd be spot on. But our guys down in Q'ute's tech lab have whipped up a way to leave behind highly encoded messages in the urine spray. Think of it kind of like a form of spy drop, a way to communicate secretly with agents in the field."

Tommy leans my way with an evil sneer smeared across his face. "But for you, little Moosie, puny as you are, they'd be more like instant Moosengers. Get it? Instant—"

"I get it," I cut him off. "Funny dog, a regular comedian. I gotta squirrel you might need to meet up with back in the 'hood…"

Tony slaps a paw down smartly on his desk, making me jump. "Okay boys, let's stay focused here. This is serious business. The future of PETSEC is at stake. Maybe even the future of pets throughout the entire Western world."

Boy, that finally got my attention. I sit up straighter in my seat and focus in on what Tony is trying to tell us. The future of PETSEC? Of the entire pet civilization, even? This must be serious! "But, Tony," I protest, the sound coming out a little bit louder and shriller than I had planned. "If it's just the president's pee-mails we're talking about, why should anyone care? After all, there couldn't be anything embarrassing in—"

"Oh, but that's just the problem, don't you see," Tony explains, leaning in. "You see, the president had more than his share of enemies out in the world.

And the PETSEC organization itself has long had folks bent on destroying everything we've been working so long to accomplish. And to fight all that perfidy, to save the world for pet democracy, sometimes we had to fight fire with fire. Get down in the dirt with them."

Ooh. I think I see the problem now. One thing I've avoided all my life is getting down in the dirt when I didn't have to. Dirt means baths. Oof! I'm shaking all over just thinking about it. Especially getting accidentally sprayed with cold water in my ears. But Tommy is talking now.

"So what you're saying is that President Boomer put something in writing that's coming back to bite him, is that it?"

"That's it on the nose, Tuxedo. And just last night we got wind of a plan by one of our enemies to release all of Boomer's pee-mails to the public. More specifically, a plot cooked up by a certain Himalayan feline named Julia Strange, the head of Kitty-Leaks. And it couldn't possibly come at a worse time, what with the election of a new president set for just two days away."

Presidential elections? That's the first time I'd heard of any of that. Or was it the second? Anyway, I usually try to steer clear of politics every chance I get. And of politicians. Talk about needing a bath…

Tommy's been chewing on his right front paw, and now looks up at Tony suspiciously. "But why do we care, Antonio? You're a shoo-in for winning the election. There's no one even lined up on the ballot to contest it."

Tony shakes his huge head, slowly. "No one up until late last night, that is. But now, right on the heels of the Kitty-Leaks announcement, we've got a new contender. From down south a ways. And I think you know exactly who I'm talking about, Moose. It's our old friend, Boss Dawg. The lead dog of the CCs. The Crimson Canines."

I think back on the last time I laid my eyes on that massive black Doberman, and my legs go limp, even as I leak a little bit uncontrollably onto the seat underneath me.

Fat Tony's Office

Tony is suddenly looking a little lost somehow, his forehead scrunched up in thought. I sneak a peek in Tommy's direction, hoping he hasn't caught wind of my—accident—but then I see him with his nose pointed my way, inhaling sharply and shaking his head in disgust, and I know I've been outed.

Tommy coughs to catch Tony's attention. "I don't know much about kitty leaks, but I can sure recognize doggie leaks when I smell it."

I try to shrink up into the smallest ball possible as Tony returns to our world.

"Wut?" he asks, looking confused for a long, long moment before he finally glances my way. "Oh. I see." He notices the red stain spreading across my muzzle and shakes his head again, warmly. "Well, nothing to be ashamed of there. Moose has every reason to be afraid, my friend. He and I went through some pretty rough moments with that gang of blood-thirsty criminals. Pretty rough moments, indeed."

He leans forward again, resting most of his weight on his two front paws. "So, here's what we're facing. We have no idea who exactly hacked the pee-mails, but it's unlikely Kitty-Leaks was behind it—they just don't have the technological know-how to make that happen. Not with the kind of encryption Q'ute's people have provided to us. And, second, it can't be a coincidence that Boss Dawg has jumped into the ring at the very last minute, and at the very same moment Julia Strange is threatening to release all the hacked info. But, with Boomer dead, what we don't know is what's in those pee-mails, and how that's going to affect the final election results in just two short days."

Tony leaves that hanging in the air while the Tuxedo and I stare at each other, trying to make sense of what role we were supposed to play in all of this. Finally, Tommy cuts his eyes back toward Fat Tony.

"And I take it the two of us are somehow part of a master plan to answer those very questions. But the bigger question is, why us? And what can we possibly do that PETSEC's Double-O agents don't already have a handle on?"

"Yeah, about that." Fat Tony suddenly jumps off the desk and returns to staring out the window, reluctant to face us it seems. "I'm afraid the Double-O's won't be of much help to us over the next few days, unfortunately," he mutters over his shoulder. "They're kind of, uh—on the sidelines at the moment, you might say."

That doesn't make any sense to me, and I say so. "On the sidelines? What do you mean by that? What mission could they possibly have that's more important than safeguarding this election? An election that's less than two days away?"

Slowly he turns back to face us, and I can't help but see the concern hanging in his dark face that speaks volumes as to how much weight he has lost over the past year.

"Moose. Tommy. We—we don't exactly have a Double-O service at the moment. All our agents have—disappeared, you might say."

Tommy and I lock eyes for what seems like an eternity, before we both turn back toward Tony, now bent over with his back pressed up against the window, staring forlornly at the floor. Like it had any answers. Tommy is the first to break the silence.

"What do you mean, disappeared? The last time I checked, there were seven feline agents on the service, all of them on their first lives. Are you saying they defected somehow?"

Tony straightens slightly, like his spine is in traction. Knew a dachshund like that, once, but I can't say I remember his name. "Defected? No, I don't think so. Not all seven of them. Especially Double-O Seven. He's on loan to us from M, the head of the United Kingdom branch of PETSEC. She swears he'd give his very life before turning his back on his Queen and country. Or our country, for that matter."

Tommy's face is twisted in angles I've never seen before as he slowly digests Fat Tony's news. "Well, if they haven't crossed over, then—" He sucks in a deep breath, trying to process everything he'd just been told. "The only other alternative is that they've been captured—"

"No." Tony jumps back up on top of the desk, back in charge again. "No way all seven of them could have been captured. Especially Bond. Double-O Seven. So that only leaves one other possibility."

"That they're dead?" Tommy blurts out incredulously. "But—how is that even possible? You said they were all on their first lives. That means they would have all been killed a total of—" He does the math quickly in his head, which I have to admit is pretty impressive. "Sixty-three times! Impossible!"

Tony shares a smile that isn't even close to a smile. "You're assuming the old wives' tale that cats have nine lives is true. Turns out that couldn't be more wrong. We cats have just one shot at life, not nine. Same as every other animal in this world."

We sit in silence for a long time, drinking this all in. Cats have only one life? That might be more earth-shaking to me than anything else I've heard out of Fat Tony today. And—far more satisfying. But Tommy Tuxedo is obviously taking the news a little harder. Probably because he's a cat.

"What do you mean, only one life? That's crazy! Fake news if I've ever heard it!"

But Tony is refusing to back down. "Crazy or not, Tommy, it's all settled science at this point, regardless of how some people might take it. Seems the whole thing was always just a myth, based upon our God-given ability to always land on our own four feet in tough situations. Plus, you gotta add in the humans' inability to really tell any of us cats apart. Sorry to have to break it too you, buddy, but once you and I hit the big one, we're burnt toast, same as anybody else. You got one life to live, so you better make the most of it."

That kind of set a damper on the whole conversation, as if any of us needed more of a wet blanket on things—which, by the way, is a saying I've never really understood, since wet blankets always have a sweet, doggish kind of smell. But, being the one animal least emotionally affected by Fat Tony's unexpected disclosure, I'm the first to step in and try to de-squirrel our discussion.

"Okay, so apparently Agents Double-O One through Seven are now off somewhere sitting in ceramic urns, waiting for their final resting place, or feeding the worms in some sinister, secret pet cemetery. So, where does that leave us? I've got din-din waiting for me at home in less than three hours, and as much as I appreciate your predicament election-wise, how exactly does that affect us pets way out in the suburbs? I mean, no offence, but PETSEC always likes to talk a big act about how they're here for us, but in the end, saving Killer and the other animals at Southside Prison came down to a grassroots effort, if you'll excuse me for saying so. Out in the 'burbs, we kind of feel like you and the other blow-hards at PETSEC might just be taking us all for granted, just expecting us to vote a certain way, regardless of whether you really give a hoot about our needs. So, I'll give you that Boss Dawg seems an unlikely hero for the PETSEC organization, but you still haven't sold me much on the alternative. Especially given what I know about the—ahem—establishment candidate." I toss Tony what I think is a meaningfully arched eyebrow.

"That's fair," Tony acknowledges, moving around the huge desk to join us, ending up standing just a few feet off to my right. "And I'll agree with you that PETSEC has in many ways lost its own way, lost its true path. We've been way too focused on the institutions of government, and not on the actual constituents of our government. Or, even more importantly, on our non-constituents, the pets and other animals we should be serving every day regardless of how they vote. Every day in every way." He seems to be examining the bottom of his left paw for a second, like maybe something's caught between his toes. "But, okay Moose, maybe now it's our time to change our ways, maybe it's finally our time to shine. With any luck, and with help from the—grassroots folks like you, folks who actually have their noses at the grass roots level each and every day—

33

PETSEC can evolve into something different, something truly great. Become a government where all of God's animals have equal rights under the law. Where we learn to serve all of the downtrodden beasts of this planet, where every single animal is protected, regardless of their abilities or economic accomplishments."

As much as I try to appreciate what Tony's trying to say, I can't help but think it sounds an awful lot like that crazy liberal guy I heard about when I was just a puppy. Carl Barks, I think his name is, going on and on about how my bone is your bone and all that. Crazy stuff, like I said. The thing is, as an Aussie I have to think back on the origins of my own people, back to a time when survival of the fittest was the only way to survive at all, and I have to believe there's gotta be some kind of middle ground in all of that. I mean, idealism versus realism, that's a concept for you. But then again, all this kind of thinking is really way above my food grade. After all, in the end I'm just a dog. My whole world pretty much boils down to bones, breakfasts and walkies. Get all three in one day and I'm one satisfied little puppy.

Suddenly I realize Tony and Tommy have been talking while I've been thinking. Not the first time that's happened, I'll assure you. Bella's always complaining I only hear half of what she's saying most of the time. But, in my defense, she yaps on almost non-stop about pretty much nothing of any consequence, so—

Tony is staring at me expectantly, like maybe he asked me a question when I wasn't paying attention. I decide to cover it up with an old trick I often use on Bella.

"Uh, I think I may be missing something here, Tony. What exactly do you mean by that?"

It seems to have worked. Tony clears his throat and repeats himself, while Tommy just rolls his eyes.

"I said, Moose, can we count on you two to work together undercover to figure out what's going on out there?"

Undercover? As a matter of fact, I love being under the covers, especially this past winter when it seemed I could never ever get the chill out of my bones. So I'm all in for that.

"Uh, sure, Tony. Whatever you need. But I must say I'm a little confused about how that's really going to help the situation. I'm still quite a bit in the dark about all of this, if you catch my drift. But, sure, I still have bed privileges with my humans, so I don't think getting under the covers will wind up being all that big a problem…"

Tommy's shaking that smashed-flat face of his and making little ticking noises with his tongue. "See, Tony? I told you it wasn't gonna work. The kid's a regular moh-ron. He has absolutely no idea what we're talking about, not a word. Like I said, working with him, he'll get us both killed, I tell ya. He's like walking into a backyard minefield with blinders on, any moment you just know you're going to wind up stepping in something really nasty."

For the first time since I walked into Tony's office, I see a little doubt creep into the old cat's eyes. Somehow I know I've done it again, missed something important and then doubled down on it by saying something truly stupid. Which is part of why Bella keeps telling me I'm not cut out for this kind of thing. That I need to just quit pretending to be somebody important and accept the fact that I'm really nothing more than a common house pet who somehow got really lucky for a day or two.

But I shake all that off. Literally, I shake it off, like I just had a bath and I'm spraying water droplets all across the room. Then, with a small growl from deep in the bottom of my stomach, I fix Tony with my best steely gaze.

"Look, buddy, I may not be the most sophisticated dog in the world, and sure, I didn't manage to run some big-city crime syndicate like this fancy two-toner here, but I think my bone-a-fidos speak for themselves. And you for one saw the whole Southside thing right up, close and personal. Who was the only dog willing to step up for Killer when everyone else was content to let him take the fall for his girlfriend's death? Who stood up to the Crimson Canines when they were threatening to gut the both of us and turn us into bite-sized appetizers? Who stood shoulder-to-shoulder with you when we went back into the heart of the Crimson gangs' territory to gather intel on what was going on with the cat crack? Who came up with the whole prison break caper, and then risked his life keeping the prison guards busy chasing his chopped-off tail while the rest of you directed all the inmates down the escape tunnel? I can assure you it wasn't a certain fat cat here who spent almost the entire time plotting how he was going to make a few quick bucks off all the sacrifices everyone else was making."

I can tell that pretty much won Tony over to my side for good, when suddenly Tommy jumps up on the desk and takes on Tony eye-to-eye. "Yeah, that's exactly what I was expecting from that arrogant little Yorkie yapper. 'Look at me! Look what I did!' That's pretty much all I've heard ever since that day at Southside Prison. Ads all over the city, bragging about what he did. Even on the back of cat food cans! And to hear him tell it, he pulled it off all by himself, none of us were even there. What an ego! The very thought of it all just makes me want to puke!"

Wow. I have no idea where all that came from. I mean, ever since the prison break I haven't talked to a single soul about what happened that day, except for a time or two with Killer and Bella, and that one long conversation I had with Tony, right here in this office shortly after it happened. But I glance over at Tony, and he's bobbing his head up and down like he agrees with the Tuxedo. So clearly I've missed more than just a few snippets of conversation, here.

Tony sits back on his haunches, looking several times like he's about to say something, then thinking better of it. Finally he rubs a paw wearily across his eyes and responds to Tommy's outburst in a low, quiet voice.

"Okay, now I get it. All the animosity you seemed to be harboring for our little Terrier buddy here. I was kind of thinking it had something to do with the old Cat versus Dog thing, or some variation on all that. Kinda hoping that's all it was. But now it seems I read the whole situation completely wrong." He squeezes his lips so hard they turn bone white, then reaches a fat paw across the desk and grasps Tommy by the shoulder. "But you got it wrong, my friend. You got it way wrong."

Tommy starts to protest, but Tony holds up his other paw to cut him off. "No, you're right about the rumors that went around almost immediately after everything happened down south. Rumors that over-emphasized some facts and some roles in the prison break while minimizing others. But you see, none of that was Moose's doing."

Tony flicks his eyes in my direction, a painful grimace slowly playing across his face. "You see, Tommy, it was all my fault. I'm the one who placed all those ads."

Fat Tony's Office

The room is suddenly deathly quiet, and you could have heard a kibble drop as Tommy and I stare at Tony, who suddenly seems to be far more interested in something happening in a distant corner of the room.

"What do you mean, you placed the ads?" Tommy looks like he's ready to come across the desk at Tony, his fangs showing, his paws twitching uncontrollably. "Why in the world would you do a stupid thing like that?"

Tony still won't look at us, but slowly the story begins to leak out, like my slobber does when I smell something really juicy. Or a bell rings.

"I guess—I guess Moose already understands some of what went down. You see..." Tony stops to clear his throat, the effort sounding more like he's gagging on something. Which maybe he is—gagging on the truth. After a few seconds, he starts up again.

"You see, this Fat Tony gig, this whole 'world's greatest cat detective' bit, it was all mostly just smoke and mirrors. I—when I first got started in this business, I played it all up completely legit. Hung out a shingle with my real name on it. Anthony Shapiro."

"Shapiro?" Tommy sputters. "But that's not an Italian name. That's—"

"Jewish. Yeah, I know. But the thing is, I wasn't pulling in any real traffic, and it got to the point where I couldn't even pay the bills. And I had racked up quite a tidy obligation to Big Ollie at the Shedd, gambling and what not, so I knew I had to make some changes. And quick, before Ollie decided to call in some of the loans. That's when I went out and hired this big high dollar marketing firm downtown, paid them good money to do a complete makeover of my PI business."

I already knew about all of this. I'd confronted Tony—Anthony—about everything, right after the prison break. But it was becoming abundantly clear this was all unwelcome news to the Tuxedo.

Tommy sits down hard on the desktop, suddenly looking completely deflated. Crushed, like his whole world had just collapsed. Which I guess it somehow had. After a long moment, he tilted his face back up toward Tony, who was still refusing to catch our eyes. "So, I'm guessing they told you—"

Tony is nodding, slowly. Painfully. "They recommended I rebrand myself as Fat Tony, a world-wise Italian with a paw into just about everything happening on the streets. Instant credibility with all the people who really counted. Potential clients. Dogs and cats with the hard cash I desperately needed. And then, right after the Southside thing, they pushed me hard to push out all that stuff, too. The ads, seemingly everywhere you turned around in the city. They thought it could bring in a boat load of new business for me. And sure, I got a few new clients out of it, but not even enough to cover my increased marketing costs. That's why, when the job at PETSEC opened up, I literally jumped at the opportunity. The opportunity to actually pull in a regular paycheck for a change, instead of always living paw to mouth."

Tommy is slowly rubbing a paw through his own whiskers, remembering. "So, when I first met you a few years back, and you sprung me out…"

Tony nodded again, his guarded eyes now flicking back and forth between Tommy and me, seeming to be carefully gauging our responses. "Yeah, I had just made the transition to 'Fat Tony' by then. Took a few language classes to pick up some useful

Italian lingo and take on a halfway believable Italian accent. When you called, it was my first chance to see if the new branding would work. Turns out it did. At least for a while."

Tommy is still rubbing his whiskers, hard. "Okay, I get the whole rebranding thing. People do it all the time. And I guess it really worked out for you in a way, made you pretty famous around these parts. Particularly after what you pulled off in Evanston—"

"Yeah, about that." Tony is back to staring off into the far corner, refusing to face us. "That whole thing about Evanston. About the Greyhounds. That was all kinda part of the rebranding, too."

Tommy stopped his paw in mid-stroke. "You mean that never happened? But it was in all the—"

"In the news. Yeah." Tony took a big gulp, like he was swallowing something big and hard that refused to go down, like that chicken bone I chomped down on that one time. Never make *that* mistake again. Tony was still explaining. "The Evanston Greyhound caper, that was a real thing. What wasn't real, though, was my part in any of it. The marketing guys, they came up with all of that."

Like I said, this was all just rechewing old kibble to me, but Tommy looked like he was taking it hard on the chin. What little chin he had.

"So, what I'm hearing here, Tony—*Anthony*--is that ninety-nine percent of the stories we've all heard about you are just plain bull hockey?"

"W-e-l-l, maybe not ninety-nine. More like eighty-five. Ninety at the most."

The office gets deathly quiet again. Tommy hops off the desk and starts pacing back and forth, the sound of his well-manicured paws striking the ground like a clock ticking away in the background. Back and forth, back and forth. Finally he stops, and turns to stare squarely at me, his eyes slightly squinted.

"So, Moose, you don't seem to be at all surprised by any of this. I take it this isn't the first time you've heard this story?"

I shake my head no, not really knowing what else to say. Tommy glances back at Tony, who now appears to be shrinking to the size of a small lost kitten, stuck on top of his desk with no place left to hide.

Tommy's voice is dripping with venom. "And, putting two and two together, *Anthony*, over the past year, your people—your *marketing* team—have been flooding the airwaves with all these stories about the Southside prison break, just so you could keep your name fresh in everybody's minds? Your second big accomplishment, after the Greyhounds? Except that, once again, you really had very little to do with any of it. All just one big stinking lie. Is that about it? Is that what I'm hearing here?"

Tony doesn't look like he's going to be talking anytime soon, so I decide to throw in a few words in his defense. "It's not like he didn't do *anything*. I mean, he helped me hunt down the Crimson Canine gang. And then he led me to you, to figure out how to break into the prison."

"I gotta respect your loyalty, Moose," Tommy says, still keeping a sharp eye on Tony over his right shoulder. "But the thing is, if I've got things right, the Crimson Canine angle turned out to be a dead end, a dark alley that ultimately led to nowhere. And it's not exactly like I'm all that hard to locate. I mean, unlike our Maine Coon cat friend here, my reputation has always been on the up-and-up in this city. I *earned* all my accolades. The hard way."

I've got to admit he's got a point, there. While Tony did help me find the CCs and figure out who killed Killer's girlfriend—and why—at the end of the day it didn't help us save Killer from being put down, even in the slightest. At the end of that day, quite literally. But that's old history, now. The real question is, where do we go from here? And what does any of this mean to our new mission? I start to say something when Tommy beats me to it.

"Okay, I guess we got all the cards on the table now." He stares meaningfully in Tony's direction, who manages to squeeze off a barely perceptible nod. "Good. No more surprises, then." Tommy leans back against his chair, staring up at the ceiling, looking for all the world like he's just escaped a mauling from a pack of wild dogs. "So, the way I see it is, we've got two problems to deal with now. First—" He flicks one claw out from a toe on his left paw. "We gotta figure out who's behind the push to get Boss Dawg elected president, which I think we can all agree would be a disaster of epic proportions. Even given the unfortunate alternative." He says that last part with a low doggish growl, as Tony and I can't help but nod our agreement. "Second." Another claw. "There's the issue of what to do about our friend *Shapiro*, here. After Boomer's death, he's now the establishment's candidate for the top job, whether we like it or not. We just don't have time over the next—" He glances out the window at the Chicago skyline, now nearing midday "—day and a half to install any reasonable alternatives. Of course, our choices would be a whole lot different right now if the powers that be had ever managed to hang something on Boss Dawg—we could have blocked his election on constitutional grounds. But he's got way too many people on his payroll making sure that never happens, so I guess that means we're going to have to dance with what brung us. If our only options at this point are a president who's a pants-on-fire liar, versus one who's a cold-blooded killer, I guess—a liar it is, you know?"

I give him my best attempt at a wry smile. "I mean, he is a politician, right, Tommy? Being a liar isn't exactly a disqualifier for the job."

"No, you're right about that, Moose." Tommy hooks a claw over his shoulder in the direction of the front door. "And we're losing valuable sunlight right now jawing about something we just can't fix at the moment. The solution to that problem will have to come later, when the election's finally over. So, for right now, we gotta find someone somewhere who can point us in the direction of this Himalayan chick, Julia Strange. And get to her before she manages to spill her guts out all over the streets of Chicago. Maybe even literally spill her guts, given everything that's at stake here…"

Just the mention of the work 'steak' sets my mouth to watering, and I'm wondering whether we might find time to scare up a little snackie or two before din-din, as I hop off my seat and race after him out the door. Leaving Tony behind, still quivering on top of the desk like a cat that got left out in the cold.

The Dead Fish Bar, 11:30 a.m.

The dilapidated sign over the equally dilapidated entrance says we're at the Dead Fish Bar, and judging from the stench that's filling my ample nostrils right about now, I'd have to say there's plenty of truth in their advertising. If anything, the place should be called the Dead Whale Bar. It's that bad.

Tommy turns to me just as we're about to enter and pulls me aside. I look up at him, gleaming brightly in the last rays of sunshine before we step inside the bar. He's the perfect specimen of a feline, tall and thin, but somehow also radiating both a physical and an inner kind of strength, his black fur and alabaster chest just screaming big money.

He lays a paw on my shoulder, softly. "Look, Moose, let's be frank with one another. This is serious business we're involved in, the kind of business that gets people hurt if they're not careful. I know Fat Tony—or whatever his name is—thought you were ready for this, but I think it's pretty obvious right now that his judgment in these kind of matters is pretty suspect…"

Part of me is offended by all this, by the suggestion that I can't handle this kind of dangerous situation. But, to be frank, another part of me is thankful for the get-out-of-jail-free card. As Bella keeps telling me, I was never really trained for this type of high-stakes undercover action. (Yes, I finally figured out what they were really talking about back then. You think I'm stupid? Duh!)

I'm just about to take him up on it when it all suddenly hits me. When I first hired Tony to look into Penny's murder, he wanted to send me home to sit on my paws, the same as Tommy. But, as it turned out, without my help, especially my unique ability to deal with the canine side of the investigation, Tony never would have gotten anywhere with the probe, and Killer would likely now be buried somewhere in a tall pile of discarded dog carcasses in the county dump, instead of lounging around safely in the warm luxury of his nice new home, probably with his new little mistress's arms wrapped tightly around his neck.

And, if anything, what's at stake here—and yeah, I figured that part out, too!—is not just one dog's life, but the safety of all pets, all across our planet. Unlike one certain female Corgi back in my

50

neighborhood, this is just not the time to Welsh on my obligations to my community. Especially since it's the same community that stepped up so bravely for me when I needed them to help me save Killer.

I give Tommy a big smile and shake my head. "Nope, gotta see this one through, Tuxedo. This is not the time to cut and run."

"Are you sure about that?" Tommy doesn't seem all that convinced. "I mean, this is Big Ollie's world we're stepping into. One wrong move from any of us and—"

Whoa! That stops me in my tracks. "Big Ollie? Isn't he the loan shark killer whale from the Shedd Aquarium, the one I almost took out a loan from back when we needed to score some explosives?" Once again, I seem to be at least one step behind everything that's happening all around me in this case. "Why should we worry about him? What we're up to, it doesn't sound like we'll need to be borrowing money anytime soon. And if we do need some cash, I'm sure PETSEC's good for it."

"No, Moose, you've got it all wrong." Tommy keeps looking back over his shoulder, nervously, like he's expecting something or someone to come barreling out the door at him any moment now. "The Big O don't just handle the consumer lending game, he's got a fin dipped into just about every racket in the big city. Dames, drugs, numbers, you name it, he runs it. And if you accidentally pull off something that runs afoul of one of his operations, costs him any dough, baked or not, then bing-bang-boom, he's got some goodfellas who'll take it all out of your fur. And I mean that literally. After they skin the fur right off your back, that is. While you're still alive. So, you still think you're really up for that kind of action, little fella?"

Whoa, again! Now I really gotta step back and think this one through again. I mean, don't get me wrong, I'm every bit as tough as the next dog—I'm an Aussie, don't you forget—but I've got other obligations to folks back in the neighborhood that I need to be considering right about now. Obligations that will clearly require me to be wearing all of my own fur, if you get my drift.

I'm just about to cave on the whole operation and head for the safety of home, when out of the blue a giant black paw lands on Tommy's shoulder from behind.

The Dead Fish Bar

I t's way too dark inside the doorway to see clearly who's snuck up behind Tommy, especially since I'm still standing out in the middle of the blazing mid-day sun, but even so it's pretty clear that whatever it is it's huge, and it's blending in way too well with the smoky stench vomiting out on top of us from inside the bar.

Tommy turns around slowly, ready to spring into action at any second. I can see the muscles on his legs tense up, all his claws now fully extended, and I crouch down into a fighting position myself. Whoever this big blob is, we won't go down easy.

And then the blob steps out into the light. And becomes the biggest, blackest cat your eyes have ever seen. "Tuxedo! Moose! What brings you two around dese parts dese days? I'd have pegged the both of you for something a little higher class!"

It's Ike! The Jamaican cat from down on the South Side, the one who helped Tony and me when we were trying to figure out who killed Penny!

I leap forward and stick out a paw. "Ike! It's really great to see you, buddy! What are you doing all the way up here? Still living in that shed next to the school?"

"Naw, haven't you heard, mon? De Fisheye and I have gone into bidness together. We're repackaging de food other places be throwing out, then cleaning it all up and selling them like new on de street. You know, like de hippies all say, recycle, renew…"

It's so great seeing him again, I can't help but grin back at him like I have the rabies or something. "Hey, that's a great idea. Get rid of all the unnecessary waste, and feed the furry folks, all at the same time!"

"An' make some good money doin' it, too. I mean, de cost of de goods approaches zero, if you get me. So it's all in de profits."

Pretty impressive, I must say. But then I always knew Ike had the smarts to really make something of himself someday. "Good for both of you! But, hey, do you remember my friend, Tommy Tuxedo? He's was there at the prison break—"

"Shore I know of him! Everyone knows the Tuxedo! Give it dere, mon!"

The two of them bump fists for a second, and Tommy and I finally let out a tense breath.

"But, seriously," Ike asks us, "what are you two doing hanging around a place like dis? Dese people, dey pretty scary folks, you know? Even I try to avoid dese kind of dives dese days. I'm only here to meet a fellow about a delivery."

Tommy takes the lead explaining what's been happening, leaning in closer. "We're here working on a thing for PETSEC. I'd tell you more, but—"

"Den you'd have to kill me," Ike responds with a laugh. "Yeah, good thing I'm not more curious, 'cause I'd like to see you and Moosie give dat a good try!"

He has a point. Ike is easily twice the size of Tommy and me put together, and it's all well-toned muscle, from the looks of what's bristling just under his fur.

Ike looks out over my shoulder and into the street. "But hey, great seeing you guys, but my mon's here, so I gotta go. Moose, don' be such a stranger. Come visit with de Fish and I some time when you get a chance. We've set up our headquarters out in dat same alley where you met him de first time. You can't miss it."

"Will do, Ike," I agree heartily with a short wave goodbye. "And give Fisheye my best. Good to see you two are doing well. Couldn't happen to a finer pair of guys, I tell you!"

With Ike now leaving us and heading out into the street, we turn and head inside the Dead Fish, the earlier question about my staying on the team now apparently forgotten.

The inside of the bar is somehow even darker than it seemed from the outside, every surface grungy with filth and leftover cigarette smoke, the floor so nasty I almost wish I had my rain booties on as we stride purposefully but stickily across the room toward the main bar.

I check out the various denizens of the room as we stroll past, careful though not to make direct eye contact with any of them. It's an odd collection of all kinds of animals, some domesticated, some very much less so, but all apparently having no place better to be on this, the first sunny day in weeks, than sitting in a flea-bitten bar tossing back foul-tasting, over-priced drinks. Not exactly this Aussie's definition of a good time.

I grab Tommy's arm to get his attention.

"Are you sure this is all that good an idea? Like Ike says, this isn't exactly our type of crowd."

Tommy gives me the kind of look you usually see folks give their paws when they've accidentally stepped in something.

"Here's the thing, Moose. If time wasn't a factor, we could play this out slowly, cast out a wide net and then throw back anything that didn't turn out all that promising. But we don't have the luxury of time, right now. We got less than a day and a half to solve this thing. Less than a day and a half to find out who's been murdering the best secret agents this world has ever seen, hacking into a pee-mail network Q'ute Branch swears is unhackable, and threatening to disrupt one of the most important elections in animal history."

He quickly studies the bar himself, and I get the impression he's not liking what he sees. "Yeah, ideally we could set out some mousetraps here and there and then sit back and relax, waiting for one of them to snap shut. But that just isn't an option for us here. We can't set any mousetraps, because we don't even know what kind of cheese to put in the traps. We don't even know if our enemy is interested in cheese, for that matter. So that leaves us with only one option. We have to *become* the cheese, we have to lure them to us. Because we already know one particular type of cheese they're going to want to come for. They are obviously fatally attracted to Double-O agents. And in just a few short weeks they've managed to eliminate the entire service, including Double-O Seven. So, if we have any chance at all of identifying who's behind all this, of finding them in time to put an end to all the mischief, we've got to set that mousetrap. We've got to spread the scent of our own particular brand of cheese far and wide. And hope our trap gets sprung long before they can finish off all the cheese. While at least one of us is still standing."

That makes sense, I have to admit, but I still can't shake the feeling that it all seems like some kind of crazy suicide mission. But by now we've reached the main bar, and Tommy motions for me to hang back a foot or so while he handles business.

The bartender looks like the unfortunate result of some kind of mixed breeding operation that went very, very wrong. His fur is spotty at best, with a scraggly-looking brown mane loosely circling his neck, his teeth a mix of yellow and black. Where he has any at all. He's wiping down a glass with a grease-smeared rag as Tommy slaps something down on top of the bar in front of him. Barkeep stares down at it, then up at Tommy, checking him out.

"Yeah, wutter yer havin?"

Tommy leans forward conspiratorially. "To start with, tuna if you've got it. Shaken, then poured."

Barkeep nods, looking distracted, then stomps down to the end of the bar, muttering all the while to himself. He scrounges around under the bar for a few moments, finally returning with a small rusted tin can with no label. Pulling a bowl out from underneath the counter in front of Tommy and wiping it out with the elbow of his shirt, he raps the can down hard on the counter, twice, then pries open the lid and pours its contents out into the bowl. From where I'm standing it doesn't look or smell all that bad, but I certainly wouldn't want to be the first to sink my eyeteeth into that particular hot mess.

"Never seen you around these parts before," Barkeep grumbles. "You gotta name?"

Tommy stares back into his eyes, unflinchingly. "Yeah. The name's Tuxedo. Tommy Tuxedo. 009."

Barkeep pulls back slightly, his eyes sweeping in a wide arc around the room. His voice is more than a little louder when he finally responds. "Ooh, we got ourselves a gen-u-wine Double-O agent here, eh? Impressive."

The eye he's giving Tommy suggests he's anything but impressed. I carefully move in a little closer, just in case something goes down quickly and I need to have Tommy's back.

Tommy flashes his trademark Tuxedo smile, a smile that must have cost him a small fortune. "Double-O in the flesh."

"And I suppose you have a license to kill, like all the others?" Barkeep asks with a sneer.

Tommy looks nonplussed. "Yes, I do, as a matter of fact. Mice mostly, the occasional bird when I get the chance." Tommy leans in even closer. "But enough with all this kissy-face small talk. I need answers, serious answers to some very serious questions, and Ollie tells me this is the place to start."

Barkeep jumps back a bit at the mention of Big Ollie's name, then he narrows his eyes.

"That's a dangerous name to be throwing around in this bar, around these people." He glances around the place again, and as I do the same, I see that virtually every eye on the bar is now focused like a laser beam on the center of our backs.

But Tommy seems oblivious to all that.

"So let's start with you telling me what you know about the missing Double-O's."

The two of them engage in some kind of mutual assured destruction stare-down contest, Barkeep absent-mindedly wiping out the inside of the same filthy glass with the same filthy rag the whole time. Finally, he appears to give up on the pointless fight and cuts his eyes toward a back corner of the bar, far from the front door or any of the bar's grime-smeared windows.

"Guy you want is back there. A Norwegian wharf rat, answers to the name Olaf. If he's answering at all, that is. Go say your peace, and if he's talking, he's talking. But listen, when you're done, you're done, then get the hell out of here. I don't need any trouble, not in my bar. And your kind always means trouble in these parts. Tuxedo."

Tommy flashes him an unfriendly smile, then gives me a quick nod and heads toward the back corner of the room where Olaf the wharf rat is waiting for us.

The Dead Fish Bar

Tommy slides into the empty seat across from the rat like he owns the place, and when Olaf doesn't respond, Tommy reaches across the table and pours the rat's beer out onto the floor beside them. The rodent is on his feet in an instant, a rusty but dangerous-looking blade held firmly in his left paw in front of him. And he's massive, kind of like the rat equivalent of my buddy Ike. A low moaning noise like a dangerous storm is slowly escaping his mouth, a noise picked up by a frighteningly large number of other denizens of the bar all around us.

"Tell me why I shouldn't just gut you right as I'm standing here?" Olaf asks in a low and scratchy voice, moving easily and quickly around the table, the blade now just inches away from Tommy's face.

Tommy doesn't flinch, but I'm making myself busy checking out any available escape routes. And finding out that the bar's remaining clientele appears to have closed them all off in a heartbeat. The bar has suddenly gone deadly quiet, and I can hear my own heart thudding loudly in my chest.

"Nice knife, little mousie," Tommy growls in response. "But didn't your mother ever tell you that's it's bad luck for little mousies to play with—mousers?"

I didn't even see the move, and I was staring straight ahead at both of them at the time. One moment the rat is lunging forward, and the next moment Tommy's behind him, pressing the business side of the knife hard into the front of Olaf's throat. And, almost immediately, everyone else in the bar seems to have lost any interest in the little drama playing out at our table and have all returned to minding their own business. But as they settle back into their seats, I notice that most of them are still watching us very carefully out of the corners of their eyes. And various weapons I hadn't seen before have now made their way to the tops of almost all of the tables.

Meanwhile, the rat is making a rather pathetic attempt to pry the knife away from his throat, but that only buys him a new line of blood now trickling down the front of his neck and onto the front of his filthy shirt. Tommy leans in, his breath tickling the rat's right ear.

"Look, rat. I only came here to get a few simple answers to a few simple questions. Nothing personal, unless you want to make it so. But I'd prefer to end this situation with your head still attached to your body. In my experience that makes it a whole lot easier for you to tell me what I need to know."

The rat is scanning the room for backup, but apparently he isn't seeing anything more than I am, so he caves pretty quickly.

"Hey, no reason to get touchy. I may have overreacted, is all. I mean, it was almost a full bottle…"

"Not a problem," Tommy tells him, relaxing his hold and returning to his seat, but keeping the knife. "You need a beer? I'll get you another." He nods over his shoulder toward Barkeep. "Perhaps I simply failed to introduce myself properly. The name's Tuxedo. Tommy Tuxedo. Double-O Nine, licensed to kill." He wags his chin in my direction. "And this here is a fellow Double-O agent. We're here to ask you a few questions about who or what is behind the recent disappearance of several of our colleagues…"

Fellow Double-O agent? This is honestly the first I've heard about any of this. But I can't really say it's a big surprise. Okay, actually, it is, but it shouldn't be, right? I mean, what dog or cat has done more in recent times to advance the interests of pets in this city? Although, to be fair, I really have next to no idea what PETSEC has done since the Southside breakout. Or before that, for that matter. So, I guess I'm back to listening.

The Norwegian is looking ill, probably because he's checking out the same room full of eye-corners I'm seeing right now, and not picking up any sign of a criminal version of a cavalry heading his way. But Tommy isn't cutting him any slack.

Just as I think the tension between Tommy and Olaf can't possibly get any worse, Barkeep shows up with a bottle of beer and slaps it in front of the rat with one eye carefully trained toward the cat.

"Put it on my tab," Tommy grumbles.

"I'll put it on your tabby hide," Barkeep tells him before turning sharply and heading back to his station, busying himself once again with wiping glasses behind the bar.

But the arrival of a new bottle of beer seems to have worked some kind of magic on the rat, as he slunks down into his chair and takes a long, slow sip.

"So, Double-O, what brings you down to my little corner of the world in such a huff?" he growls, in a squeaky kind of way.

Tommy is busy spinning the knife in the center of the table. "I think you know very well why we're here. Like I said, the Double-O service is suddenly short a few members, and I'm not leaving this place until I find out who's behind all that. And why."

Olaf considers Tommy's words for a few moments as he sips thoughtfully on his beer. "And why exactly do you think I can help out with any of that? I'm just a common rodent, after all, minding my business out on the docks, same as any other."

"Because word on the street is, if you need to ferret out some down-and-dirty info on what's going down in this city, then the Norwegian's the best place to start."

Olaf suddenly sits up straighter, his eyes bright. "Oh, you want the Ferret? Well, why didn't you say so in the first place? He don't come around here anymore, his place of business is down at the Carving Knife, closer to the warehouse district. Or so I'm told. Personally, we rodents try to avoid that particular place any chance we get. You know…"

Oh great. Now I'll have that stupid children's tune stuck in my head for the rest of the day. I shake my head vigorously to try and knock it out, causing my two tablemates to stare sharply at me like I've lost my mind. Which I probably will at some point if I get stuck with 'Three Blind Mice' running nonstop through it all afternoon long…

Tommy finally turns back to face Olaf. "I don't want the Ferret, you stupid rat! Ferret's just an expression for—" He stops and shakes his head slowly, realizing the futility of trying to reason with a creature that has a brain the size of an English pea. If that. Tree rats or wharf rats, they're all the same. Pretty much all a rat is useful for is getting some inside info and spreading the Black Plague. Tommy tries again, holding the knife up in the air in front of him, the blade catching a ray of light from a dingy window on the far side of the bar and glimmering menacingly. "What I'm saying, rat, is you want to get out of this bar with your tail still attached to your sizable hairy butt, you better start talking. Who's behind the attacks on PETSEC?"

Olaf's eyes dance around the room as he does a quick calculus on the situation. Which doesn't take long—for a rat, even adding one plus one is way above their education level. "Listen up, cat, I'm no stool pigeon—"

Tommy scowls and drives the point of the knife deep into the center of the table, leaving it quivering between them. "You'll be feeding the pigeons within the hour if you don't start talking. And I don't mean scattering seed. Listen, rat, I'm running out of time, here. And patience. So spill it, who's behind all the whacking and hacking?"

Olaf pauses, thinking, then peels the label off his beer and scratches out two words before shoving it across the table toward Tommy. "There. That should get you headed in the right direction. But let's all be clear, here. I didn't say a single word, right? Not one single word. I gotta reputation to maintain."

Tommy glances down at the label, then spins it around so I can read what's scrawled across it. Just two simple words. Russian Wolfhounds. My stomach turns over again as sweat breaks out across my forehead. The Russians! For the third time today I'm seriously reconsidering my role in this whole operation. In the long run, it might be better to live with Boss Dawg sitting at the head of PETSEC than wind up swimming around in a steaming bowl of beet soup. Because that's pretty much the only two options I'm facing right now. Be lucky to somehow make it through the rest of this day alive, or else skedaddle back home so I can live to die another day. And I do hate beets.

Downtown Chicago,
12:45 p.m.

T ommy's jumping in and out of traffic so fast I can barely keep up, and more than once I missed getting run over so close the driver stopped and checked under his car for my dead body. And I gotta tell you I'm happy they didn't find me.

I holler out to Tommy to slow down, but he doesn't seem to be hearing me, and instead just doubles down on his pace. I'm just about to give up on this crazy high-speed chase when suddenly he stops dead in his tracks and studies a wall on one of downtown's tallest skyscrapers, just a few doors down from the Sears Tower, or whatever they're calling it these days.

"Only been here once," he mumbles under his breath, still not paying me any mind.

"What are we looking for, Tommy?" I ask in between hacking gasps for air, squeezing in closer to see what he could possibly be looking for on an apparently unremarkable stretch of blank brickwork.

Tommy starts feverishly pawing at the bricks, and I'm beginning to think the tuna he ate back at the Dead Fish might have been tainted after all, when abruptly he stops in mid-paw and steps back, a smile now creasing his black-and-white face.

"Ah, little Moosie, haven't lost my touch after all. Stand right there." He points to a position on the sidewalk just to the right of where I'm standing, and I hold my questions for the moment as I move over to do as he says. Tommy presses one last brick, then hops over to stand right next to me, almost touching. And he lands there just a split second before the ground opens up underneath our feet and swallows us alive.

Down the Rabbit Hole

We plunge through the endless darkness for what seems like an eternity, and I'd like to say I'm taking the whole thing like a proper Double-O agent. Except that Tommy is here as a witness, so I'll have to admit that maybe, just maybe, I let out a squeak or two along the way. Okay, Tommy might say it was more than just a squeak, something more on the order of a scream, or even a terrified, blood curdling shriek. But you know how Tommy exaggerates all the time, so let's just leave it at a few squeaks for now.

Anyway, after an eternity has passed, or maybe just five or ten seconds—it's hard to tell when you're busy free-falling straight to your death—a bright light comes on right beneath our feet, starting as just a pinpoint, then swelling to the size of a giant glowing mouth, and we fall into it without slowing one bit. My eyes are squeezed tight as a deer tick, waiting for the inevitable, and I can just feel the first pale rays of doggie heaven hitting my cheeks, when I slam paws-first into something else instead. Something soft, something that gives way for just a fraction of a second before bouncing me right back up a few feet or so toward the sidewalk stretching high above my head. I fall back, then bounce up one or two more times. Finally, I gulp down the contents of my stomach that have been desperately trying to find their own escape route, then bravely pry open my eyes and see that I'm lying on top of a large net in the middle of an otherwise empty room. Tommy is already brushing off the shoulders of his jacket and is jumping down to the floor, about a foot or so beneath my feet.

"Come on, Moose. We don't have all day." He's moving briskly toward a plain gray door set in the far wall as I manage to finally pull myself together enough to jump down to ground level to join him. And never in my life has the ground felt sweeter under my paws.

Q'ute Branch, 1:00 p.m.

The plain gray door leads into an equally gray tunnel, dimly lit by small LED strips set into the walls at about eye level to me. My paws are feeling a little wobbly after the long fall, and I think I may have twisted something important when I hit the net, but hey, I'm a professional here, so I'll just have to fight through the pain.

"Hey, Tommy," I call out to my partner, who's still taking the lead, walking several steps in front of me like he is on some kind of mission. Which I guess he is. "What you said about me being a Double-O agent. Is that for real? And what number do I get? Double-O Ten?"

Tommy turns and shoots me the same long look he'd been using on Olaf the Rat, his eyes rolling upward in their sockets. I quickly check the ceiling myself to see if there's anything up there I might have missed, but it's just plain gray like everything else.

"Double-O Ten? Really? Just how does that make any sense?" He shakes his head. "No, Moose, the only double o's you'll likely ever get is when people say 'oh no' every single time you come around."

It takes me a second or two to figure out what he just said, and then he's already turned back around and is walking quickly toward the end of the tunnel before I can figure out a response. Is that really what everyone says about me behind my back? "Oh no?" After everything I did springing all of the dogs and cats out of Southside prison last year? And putting my own fur-covered hide squarely on the firing line in the process?

But Tommy's getting way ahead of me, so I drop it for now and rush to catch up.

At the far end of the tunnel is another plain gray door. Tommy turns the knob and pushes it open without hesitation, and a brilliant light pours into the tunnel, blinding me for a second.

As things finally come back into focus, I step forward into the largest room I've ever seen, and all I can say is that it kinda looks like the Ringling Brothers Circus has met the front lines of a high-tech World War Three! There's chaos everywhere I see. Off to my right, a large dog is getting shot out of a canon, and just before he splats into the wall on the far side, a rocket pack on his back ignites and he stops almost on a dime, hovering in mid-air for a moment before slowly easing to the ground. Off to my left, a gang of monkeys is busy throwing some kind of brown, nasty-looking substance at a line of human-shaped mannequins, and wherever the brown stuff hits the mannequins they let off a greenish cloud of gas and immediately start to dissolve. A few steps further on I pass a common tabby wearing a bright blue collar. Out of nowhere a pack of robotic Rottweilers pounce on the cat, only to be thrown back by some kind of bright blue force field that has sprung out from the collar, completely surrounding the cat, who's now busy licking a front paw like nothing ever happened.

It's like that all around the room, animals flying through the air, strange looking guns, a Pomeranian with no hind legs in a tiny motorized wheelchair—oh, wait, that totally makes sense—and an English Setter getting ready to bite down on a chew stick, and then suddenly spitting small red pellets out the end of the stick, blowing the heads right off another line of mannequins! I barely know where to look next, and I'm kind of frozen in my tracks, taking it all in, when I glance down and see Tommy motioning for me to join him in a small alcove set deep into the far wall. I hurry to catch up, while still being very careful not to step in front of any exploding pellets or whatever it was those monkeys were tossing around.

Tommy's already taken a seat at a table set in the very middle of the alcove as I finally arrive, slightly out of breath, whether from the strain of running or the strain of dodging all the life-threatening activities along the way it's hard to say. Sitting calmly at the far end of the table is the smallest Collie I think I've ever seen, wearing a pair of glasses with thick, Coke bottle lenses. But somehow the glasses seem to fit—her?— very well. I've only seen a Collie once or twice, from a distance at the dog park near my house, but every masculine bone in my body is instantly on full alert.

Tommy clears his throat. "Moose, this is Q'ute, head of PETSEC's special weapons, espionage and tactics team. SWEATT, for short."

Pleased to meet you," I say, sticking out a paw. "Can't say I ever met a Collie before…"

Tommy clears his throat again, but Q'ute simply smiles as she bumps my paw with hers. "Actually, Moose, you still haven't. I'm a Shetland Sheepdog, commonly called a Sheltie. But I'm honored to finally meet you, as well. Your exploits down on the South Side of our fair city are quite legendary, I must say. When we get a chance, after all this ugliness is behind us, maybe we can share some kibble sometime and you can tell me all about it."

Tommy is looking like he's just been slapped, and leans in to change the subject. "Yeah, well, let's get back to business, shall we?" He casually tosses the beer bottle label we got from the Norwegian rat onto the table. "I gotta snitch in one of the dive bars down near the Navy Pier that tells me the Russians have moved into town. Think that might be a good place to start."

Q'ute's glasses have slipped down her snout just a hair, and she pauses to push them back, giving her a long moment to absorb Tommy's news. "The Russians? Well, isn't that interesting…" She starts tapping furiously on the surface of the table, and I lean over to see that there's some type of computer screen and keyboard embedded deep inside of it. After about a minute and several mumbled comments to herself, Q'ute finally sits up straight and catches my eye.

"Well, Mr. Moose, you certainly have a knack for attracting trouble. A danger magnet of the worst kind, I must say."

That doesn't sound at all good, and I notice Tommy starting to squirm around in his seat out of the corner of my eye. The first time I've ever seen Tommy nervous. I plaster on my best smile, even as I'm busy sucking in my gut. Did I mention that Q'ute was—well—really cute?

"Trouble?" I manage to blurt out. "What kind of trouble are we talking? Sent to bed for the evening with no din-din, or getting your throat ripped out by a pack of Dobermans trouble?"

Q'ute smiles back comfortingly, but her eyes tell me otherwise, even hidden behind those thick lenses. "I think you might be better off taking on the Crimson Canines single-handedly, versus what's in store for all of us over the next few days." She slaps a paw on the tabletop in front of her, and instantly a huge computer screen lights up on the wall right behind her head. "We've had our eye on this group for quite some time, a gang of Russian Wolfhounds based out of St. Petersburg, from what we can gather. They call themselves SPECTER, shorthand for their real name, the Secret Protectorate Ensuring Canines' Total Enslavement by Russia. They're all that remains of the old KGB, the Kanine Globalist Bureau."

My fears start to melt away immediately. "Canine Globalists? That sounds like a great idea! We dogs are some of the most worldly animals out there, you know. Not like cats, who are pretty much all isolationists…"

Tommy picks this moment to speak up, his face now twisted into a fierce knot. With either fear or rage, or maybe a combination of both. "No, you idiot! It's the KGB! They have a reputation for being the most brutal, repressive group of animals anyone could ever imagine. The last thing they want is a world where every animal joins paws, singing together in a perfect three-part harmony. They're trying to turn the world into one giant concentration camp, with them playing the role of the prison guards. And in the process they're planning to exterminate almost every animal in the non-canine animal world. Starting with cats."

I glance over at Q'ute, who's nodding her head in agreement. "Yes, my friends, in the recent past the KGB was easily the most powerful agent for evil in the entire world. But there were certain political changes in Russia that took out the old guard of political idealists, and replaced them with a new guard of criminal opportunists, with SPECTER at the very center of it all. And now it seems like they've landed right here in Chicago, just two days before the most important presidential election in PETSEC history. That can't be a coincidence."

"The president, President Boomer—" Tommy sputters.

Q'ute cocks her head sideways a bit, her Coke bottle glasses shifting ever so slightly in the process. "Exactly what I was thinking. I'll have to go back and check the autopsy results one more time, but I'll bet you kibbles to canned food we'll find some type of neurotoxin hiding out somewhere in his bloodstream. A Russian neurotoxin, to be precise."

"You mean they *killed* him?" I blurt out, quickly realizing just how stupid that must make me seem to these two well-seasoned professionals. Maybe Tommy was right, after all. Maybe I am way out of my league. Treading in waters where no dogpaddle is going to save me.

"It sure looks that way," Q'ute answers, turning back to her keyboard and typing away. "We don't know a lot about the inner workings of SPECTER— they're one of the most secretive organizations on the planet—but the best intel we do have says they're headed up by this guy." One quick paw pat and instantly a picture of a particularly ugly feline flashes up on the wall behind her.

She turns her head to stare unblinkingly at the picture. "This is Vladimir Kitin, a long-time agent of the old KGB, and possibly one of the most brutal felines you will ever meet."

Now I am totally confused by all this. "But—but, he's a *cat*! I thought Tommy said the KGB—"

Q'ute turns back to peer at us over the top rim of her glasses. "Was a dogs only organization," she finishes for me. "Well, yes it was. And now, so is SPECTER. With just one singular exception. And that's what scares us all so much about this guy. A cat leading an organization dedicated to killing all cats, all around the globe? He must be quite ruthless, indeed."

I stop to study my new enemy, plastered up on the computer screen wall almost ten times life-size. "But what's up with his chest? That's got to be one of the grossest things I've ever seen. And I've seen my humans stark naked on more than one occasion, so I know my way around gross—"

Q'ute's smiles have turned pretty grim over the last few minutes, and she's wearing one of her worst right now. "Mind you, we don't have a lot of intel on Kitin, just rumors, mostly. And it's sometimes hard to separate the truth from lies he's cooked up himself just to puff up his image. But here's what we think we do know…"

Q'ute Branch, 1:30 p.m.

A quick paw click, and a map of Russia fills the wall in front of us. Q'ute quickly zooms in, focusing in on a small section of the country in the far southwest corner. "We believe Kitin was born roughly ten years ago in an area near the now-abandoned town of Pripyat, in northern Ukraine. That was the site of a catastrophic nuclear accident that took place back in 1986, a meltdown and explosion at the Chernobyl Nuclear Power Plant. It wasn't actually a nuclear explosion per se, but the resulting uncontrolled destruction of the plant spread deadly radioactive material across more than 100,000 square meters, and less lethal but still dangerous radioactive isotopes across all of Europe."

That completely floored me. "Wow! So I guess they evacuated the entire area, including the animals, right?" This was the first I'd heard of any of this. The Churnable Nucular plant? And I don't know how big 100,000 square meters is, but it had to be most of a neighborhood, at least. Maybe several neighborhoods. "So how did Kitin's family get left behind?"

"That's just the thing, Moose," Q'ute explains. "At first, the Russians didn't evacuate anyone. They just pretended nothing at all had happened, until workers at a nuclear energy plant in Sweden started showing up with radioactive dust on their clothing. The Swedes were quite fastidious about that sort of thing, and it didn't take them long before they determined the suspect nuclear material was blowing into Sweden from the Ukraine. Once the cat was out of the bag, so to speak, the Russians finally fessed up and started evacuating Pripyat and the surrounding area. Evacuating the humans, that is. The animals they mostly left behind to fend for themselves."

That news hit me in the gut like a sucker punch. "You've got to be kidding me! That's—that's—inhuman! Even for them!"

Q'ute nods, a sour look now smeared across her face. "I'd have to agree with you, Moose. Nevertheless, that's how they handled the crisis. And, even worse, they didn't completely abandon the area, even the humans. They left large numbers of soldiers behind to attempt a cleanup operation, and a skeleton staff of humans stayed behind for many years to run the one remaining nuclear plant that was still operational at Chernobyl, a plant they continued to operate for almost fifteen years. So, as incredible as it seems that they turned their backs on all the animals, they clearly valued the electricity the remaining plant provided over the lives of even their fellow humans."

Tommy finally speaks up. "Skeleton staff? I bet they were all just a bunch of skeletons after being exposed to all that radiation. But—" He motions for Q'ute to put Kitin's picture back on the wall. "Clearly, as deadly as the radiation was, some of the animals still managed to survive—"

"They did," Q'ute agrees. "And I'd show you some of the pictures from all that, but seeing as how it's just after lunch—"

"Yeah. Let's skip that, why don't we? But still, this Kitin fellow, what happened to him?"

Q'ute uses a laser pointer to circle Kitin's chest on the wall screen, and I'm glad there weren't any cats present in the room, or we'd have had a catastrophe of our own. Just saying.

"Vladimir Kitin is a member of a feline breed commonly referred to as Russian Blues, very popular in that country. Russian Blues are characterized by distinctively bright green eyes, pinkish lavender or mauve paws, and two layers of short thick fur topped by a blue-grey coat."

Kitin's paws aren't visible in the picture, but his eyes were very striking and extremely green, and the fur below his waist was thick and very blue. But above the waist was a completely different story. His chest, arms and face were completely bald, like he'd been in a bad fire or something. I tell her so.

"Yes, well, something obviously went amiss with his upper body hair, but we don't think it was a fire that caused it. More like radiation-induced alopecia, or a genetic defect that popped up in his family due to all the background radiation. But whatever caused it, Kitin appears to have embraced his baldness, and he runs around half-naked every chance he gets. Wears it like a badge of honor, I suppose."

Well, he may be proud of it, but I hope I never catch any of that alley peaches stuff, is all I'm saying. I mean, I don't like to brag or anything, but you can ask anyone, I'm one good looking canine, that's for sure.

But Tommy's talking again. "So he emerges from the radiation zone, and somehow signs up as a field agent in a violent dogs-only evil syndicate. How exactly did that work out?"

Q'ute nods and throws up a small organization chart on the wall. "Apparently, the KGB was not completely dogs-only after all. As you can see, they maintained small splinter cells employing a variety of other types of animals. We think the other animals joined because they'd been promised some kind of protection in the end, when the KGB took over the world. Or maybe they had family members being held hostage back in Russia. At any rate, these non-canine agents were critical to gathering intelligence on other groups of animals, intelligence that was then critical to the organization's long-term goal of systemic world-wide genocide. To wiping out all the other animals who could ever challenge the global canine hegemony. Dogs ruling the entire world."

Tommy is rubbing his chin. "So that was Kitin's entry point, and he used that to leverage himself to the very top of the entire organization. The top of SPECTER. He has to be pretty ruthless, indeed."

"Yes," Q'ute agrees. "He's apparently left a long and bloody trail all the way from Moscow to St. Petersburg. And now—to our fair town."

Tommy's still rubbing, lost in thought. "So what is his real game plan, then?" he mumbles, mostly to himself. "And how does that all tie into Boss Dawg throwing his collar into the ring to fill President Boomer's shoes?"

"Yeah, and why did you say this is the most important election in PETSEC history?" I ask, mostly to myself.

Q'ute flicks a paw in Tommy's direction. "I think you can answer that question better than anyone."

I turn to face Tommy dead-on. He's stopped rubbing his chin now and has both paws laid flat on the table in front of him. "Well, that's a long and complicated story to work through, but I'll give you a quick synopsis. Uh, I don't know how much you've kept up on all the politics within PETSEC—"

A quick shake of my head answers that question. I've been pretty much out of the loop regarding any kind of animal-on-animal political in-fighting my entire life, and I'd pretty much like to keep it that way. Tommy goes on.

"As you know, Moose, Fat Tony is set to break through a glass ceiling at PETSEC that has existed ever since the organization was first founded. For well over a hundred years, every single president of our organization has been a canine. There's never once been a feline—or any other breed of animal—serving in that position. Or even as vice president. No exceptions. And over time that has resulted in a significant rift in the organization, a resentment of the historical canine leadership by all the other animals, animals who feel they've all been left out in the cold, their unique needs largely ignored."

"And now a cat is finally up for election," I suggest. "Fat Tony."

"Exactly. It's a move many are hoping will help mend some of the broken fences that have been accumulating over the years, help cure a kind of cancer that's been eating away at the agency. A cancer that's contributed greatly to the rise of organizations like the KGB and SPECTER, I might add. And the eventual collapse of long-standing relationships between the various PETSEC offices all around the world."

"And you really think Tony's the answer?" I ask, thinking back to all of Tony's blatant double-dealing.

Tommy shakes his head ruefully. "I'll grant you he's not the perfect candidate. And he's probably not the candidate I would have chosen. Especially now, after our conversation earlier today. But—he's the only candidate all the other cats can rally behind. They've made it a clear cat versus dog issue. So I guess we dogs and cats don't really have a choice right now. The only other option left to us is to throw in for some other non-dog breed. A rat, maybe. Or a squirrel."

Just the thought of a squirrel running PETSEC sends a shiver down my spine. For the second time today. So, okay, I get it. There are worse alternatives than having Antonio Shapiro running PETSEC for the time being, until a better option can step up to the plate for us. "So, Tommy, Q'ute, how exactly does Boss Dawg figure into all of this? And why is SPECTER suddenly showing up in our back yard, just days before the elections?"

Q'ute flicks off the computer wall projection and sits quietly for a few seconds, thinking. "Before Boss Dawg entered the race unexpectedly, Fat Tony was the only candidate running, so he was a shoo-in for the job. And that was all carefully planned. You see, the dogs have a small but significant electoral edge

91

over the cats and all the other animals in PETSEC, and it's hard to nail down exactly how any of them will wind up voting, whether they'll stay on board with the idea of a cat at the top of PETSEC's global operations, or remain committed to the old, ultimately self-destructive status quo. In fact, according to the latest polls there are a great many dogs out there who think things have gone way too far in terms of animal equality, equal rights for all animals, regardless of breed or gender. A frighteningly large percentage of canines would actually like to roll things back a little, return to the so-called glory days when they were the undisputed lords of back yards everywhere on the planet. So—with Boss Dawg's name on the ballot, and SPECTER clearly making some kind of play to disrupt the election, Fat Tony's chances of winning are rapidly evaporating, even as we speak."

"So that just means we gotta stop talking about all this, and start doing something," Tommy says, pushing his chair back and standing up.

But I'm not quite ready to leave just yet. I still have a few more questions for Q'ute.

"Much as I'd like to hit the ground chasing after cars, the problem I'm having is where exactly do we need to start chasing. Which car exactly do we target? And, even if we manage to find these Russians, what then? From what you've just explained all too clearly, these are some pretty bad dudes we're messing with, worse than the Crimson Canines even, and I barely escaped that group of trained killers with my fur still intact, so there's that. Anyone got any ideas on how we're ever going to survive the day?"

"Short and to the point, Moose," Q'ute notes, and I quickly decide not to take that the wrong way. Tommy's sitting back down now, and Q'ute is busy popping an image of a medium-sized long-haired black canine up on the wall.

"This is a very recent picture we have of Julia Strange, the founder and titular head of Kitty-Leaks. As you can clearly see, she is a rather striking example of a classic Himalayan feline."

I couldn't really tell a marmalade cat from any other fluffer feline, but I decide to keep that to myself for now. Anyway, Q'ute is still talking.

"Strange is a fugitive from justice, wanted by several European countries, but currently she's hiding out in the Consulate General of Ecuador, located on Wabash Avenue about halfway between the river and

Millenium Park. My best guess is, the Russians are behind the hacking of our pee-mails—they're pretty much the only group capable of cracking our encryption—and as part of their dirty tricks they'll be trying to get the hacked pee-mails to Strange and Kitty-Leaks, to be distributed to the media just in time to embarrass PETSEC and Fat Tony right before the polls open on Tuesday. They'll probably target the transfer of the stolen files for sometime late Monday. That's the way I would do it, early enough to affect the outcome of the vote, but last minute enough to prevent us from mounting any kind of an effective response."

"But—what could possibly be on those pee-mails that would make any difference?" I ask, still completely perplexed by all this.

Q'ute cuts her eyes in Tommy's direction. "Uh, I'm not sure I can say. It's all pretty top-secret stuff, details about our plans to manipulate the election to make sure a cat finally wins, and about certain—peculiarities regarding Tony's background. I just know about some of it because I had to go back in and pore over all the backups after the data breach…"

"Moose knows," Tommy assures her. "And so do I, for that matter. Fat Tony fessed up earlier today."

Relief washes across Q'ute's face. And something else. Something a little foul, like maybe what she saw in the pee-mails didn't exactly sit well with her.

"Okay, well then both of you know that Tony's not exactly who he's been made out to be. And 'made out' is a pretty accurate description of what actually happened to create his public persona. But I think you can see how that story might not play out well with the general electorate. Especially an electorate that has its own reasons to distrust a cat. Reasons going back thousands of years, if not longer…"

Tommy cuts in sharply. "Yeah, that the establishment candidate is about as Italian as SpaghettiOs. And how the closest he's ever been to a hero is at the sandwich shop." Tommy stands up again, getting ready to leave. "But the sad truth is, our only alternative to Anthony Shapiro right now is Boss Dawg. Who I'm sure has worked out some kind of sweet deal with the Russians, to somehow split the power between them. And split the city, too. So I guess that means it's time to hold our collective noses and vote for the lesser of the two evils, and live to die another day."

Q'ute flicks her tail in agreement and stands up herself. "I guess your first target, then, would be the Ecuadoran Consulate, where Julia Strange has taken refuge. But—before you go, I've got a few toys my people have dreamed up that might help to balance the scales a bit between you two and the Russians. If only a little bit."

"Every little bit helps, at this point," Tommy tells her. "Even the smallest edge might spell the difference between success—or death. And personally, I'd much prefer the former."

I'm kinda hoping for success myself at this point. Seriously going with curtain number one.

Ecuadorian Consulate, 2:30 p.m.

I'm not exactly sure what I was expecting from the Ecuadorian Consulate, but a mid-sized office building right across the street from a Dunkin' Donuts was clearly not it.

We're standing right in front of the donut shop, hiding behind an electrical pole and checking out the front entrance with a dental mirror. "So, Tommy, it seems we won't have to scale some twenty-foot walls to get in after all. Easy peasy."

"Yeah, but also easy peasy for the Russians. And a twenty foot wall would have at least given us a chance to jump the Russkies from outside of the consulate. Now things could get a little more dicey."

I hadn't thought of that angle. I suppose that's why Tommy's the superhero on this particular mission, and I'm just his trusty little sidekick. In the meantime, Tommy seems to have come to some kind of decision on how best to proceed from here.

"Okay, doesn't look like we've got much choice, we've gotta head inside and reconnoiter the place up close. But that presents us with a rather large problem. I'm experienced enough in spycraft to get in and out with nobody being the wiser. But a dog and cat going in together, that's a whole 'nother kettle of fish."

I'm not really sure what a pot full of fish has to do with any of this, but I can see Tommy's concerns about the two of us just strolling in, side by side, like two thousand years of dogs and cats being mortal enemies never happened.

"Okay, Tommy, I agree. Why don't you go in first and check things out on the ground. Or, rather, check things out four floors up. Meanwhile, I'll hang out here and keep a sharp eye out for any Russians that might try and sneak inside."

"Good plan, Moose. I'll be back in a few. If you don't hear from me in thirty minutes, though, don't try and be a hero or something stupid like that. Get back to HQ and line up reinforcements. Got that?"

I wag my tail okay, even though I'm not totally buying off on that idea. I mean, if Tommy gets himself in serious trouble up there, the longer we wait to rescue him the worse his chances are of getting out in one piece. If I learned anything from the Southside Prison caper, it's that you've got to keep your options flexible if you're gonna have any hope of succeeding. Like that ancient Shar-pei philosopher once pointed out, no battle plan survives first contact with the enemy. Or at least I think it was a Shar-pei. Could have been a long-haired dachshund, now that I think about it…

So I'm hunkered down now, watching the front of the building like Max, my Great Pyrenees buddy. But, to be honest, there's not much to watch, really. The Dunkin' Donuts shop is getting way more traffic than the consulate building. And it's not even breakfast time.

Oops. That was a big mistake. One thought of breakfast, and already my stomach is grumbling. I knew I should have packed a snack before heading downtown this morning. Happens every time, you get busy—

"You see anything suspicious, Moose?"

Wha! I spin around, and immediately I see Tommy standing just a few feet behind me, leaning casually up against a pole. "How did you—"

Tommy is smirking at having caught me off-guard like that. "Just like I thought. Lost in your daydreams. What was it? Dreaming of a bone?"

No way I'm going to give him the satisfaction of answering his little sarcastic questions. And, no, it wasn't a bone, I'll have you know. It was a king-sized bowl piled high with canned food. With leftover tidbits from my humans' dinner stacked up on top, I decide to fight fire with fire and go on the offensive, instead.

"Very funny. I knew you were there the whole time. Just couldn't take my eyes off the entrance. And let the Russians sneak in while I was watching you instead."

Tommy doesn't seem totally sold on my story, so I shift gears. "So, more important at the moment, what if anything did you find out upstairs?"

Tommy's still watching me askance with those squinty little eyes of his, and takes his time to answer. "The front door to the consulate is going to be a problem. They've got two-tiered security, a door up front and a single door leading to the back, with a no-man's land in between. Or a no dog and no cat land in this particular instance. So that kinda puts a kibosh on trying to sneak in the direct way. And the fourth floor, that's a little too high up for scaling the walls and climbing in through an open window, even for a cat. Which leaves us with only one remaining option."

"Yeah, what's that?" I ask, now fully intrigued.

Tommy tells me there's apparently some kind of dumbwaiter that runs from the basement all the way up to the top floor. Too tiny for even the smallest human to squeeze in for a ride up to the consulate, but more than big enough for the two of us.

I shrug my shoulders. Do we really have an alternative, here? "Let's ride."

Ecuadorian Consulate, 3:00 p.m.

As it turns out, catching a ride on the dumbwaiter isn't as easy as Tommy first made it out to be. First of all, the button to send the thing up is mounted on the wall outside, and the door to the dumbwaiter has to be closed and locked before it will operate. That meant we had to rig up a way to push the button even after we were locked inside of the thing, but after a series of trial runs using some string, an old mop and a stack of boxes, we were finally able to get it all to work. Kind of reminded me of my old Irish Setter buddy, MacGyver. Sometimes in these situations you just have to be resourceful.

It was kind of tight inside the little elevator, Tommy being a bit larger than your average alley cat, but a long minute or so later the dumbwaiter finally came to a stop on the fourth floor, and we unlocked the door and jumped out.

We catch a big break at this point—as it turns out the dumbwaiter opens up inside a small snack bar near the back of the consulate, and no humans are standing around at the moment to see us suddenly pop out into the room from a hole in the wall. Tommy immediately rushes to the door leading into the hallway to peek out, making sure the coast is clear, then turns back to discuss next steps.

"Okay, the big question now is, where are they hiding Julia Strange?"

"I don't see how we can figure that out from in here," I suggest in a low voice. "Since we're at the very back of the consulate, I guess our best course of action is just to move forward, slowly and cautiously, until we see something that looks suspicious. If we're spotted along the way, then my recommendation is just to own the situation, act like we're supposed to be here, the way Tony taught me how to ride the elevated trains and buses."

"I like that," Tommy whispers back. "You know, Moose, we might just make a secret agent out of you, after all." He pauses to glance quickly back out into the hallway. "Okay, out of here and to the left. If our plan does fail and everything goes topsy turvy for us out there, let's plan to meet up back here and we'll see what we can figure out with the dumbwaiter. I saved some extra string for us, just in case."

Tommy goes first, slipping soundlessly into the hall with me following right on his heels. Coming to the first open doorway, he slides an eye around the bend, then shakes his head and, pointing a paw straight ahead, darts quickly past the door. I follow in quick pursuit.

We repeat that maneuver several more times before Tommy finally pulls back sharply from scoping out a room, a big smile spreading across his face. "Bingo! It's her. Julia Strange in the flesh!"

My legs suddenly go all tingly on me. You gotta love it when a plan finally comes together. Tommy slips across the doorway and pauses on the other side, gazing back at me. Holding up three outstretched claws, he counts down three, two, one, and then we both rush the room together, Tommy stopping for just a brief moment to close the door behind us. One thing I learned the hard way long ago— privacy is precious at a moment like this.

Julia Strange's Suite, 3:15 p.m.

O ther than our target, Kitty-Leaks empresario Julia Strange, we're all alone in the little room. There's a small bed set up in one corner, and a pile of Chinese takeout gathering roaches on a table off to our right. Strange is scrunched up in a La-Z-Boy recliner, watching a home-flipping show on television, and doesn't even notice us as we slip into the room.

Tommy points to a laptop computer —or is it a lapdog top?— sitting on a nightstand beside the bed. Moving quicker than I ever thought was possible, he snatches it off the nightstand and stashes it away deep beneath the bed, where only the two of us have any chance of getting to it without moving all of the furniture in the little room around.

With Strange's only apparent connection to the outside world—and, more specifically, the Internet— now fully neutralized, it's time for us to introduce ourselves to the enemy.

Tommy goes first, pushing off against the nightstand in a long arching leap that lands him squarely in the middle of her lap. Strange starts to erupt with a long and almost certainly very loud scream, but Tommy slams both front paws over her mouth, stifling the noise. Meanwhile, I come racing around the La-Z-Boy and jump right up on a coffee table sitting between her and the blaring television.

Now that I've got a closer look at her, I'll have to admit she's not all that bad appearance-wise, if you happen to have a thing for grumpy-looking marmalade cats, that is. She has chocolate, almost black paws and ears and a matching chocolate face, but the rest of her is more like white chocolate. Her face is all smashed in, flat even for a cat, and her eyes are staring right at us with almost no white showing around the edges.

Meanwhile, Tommy's wasting no time getting into it with her, switching to Doglish, which she at first pretends not to understand. But of course she has to be pretty fluent in American Doglish, since she's evidently been in constant contact with the Russians about all of our pee-mails. And, not to overstate the obvious, she's a dog. Finally, realizing we're not buying in to any of her heated denials, she caves in.

"What do you want?" she demands in a thickly accented voice. "Why are you here? Are you connected to the Wolfhoonds? To Vladimir Kitin?"

"Do I look like a Wolfhound to you, lady?" I ask while Tommy is frantically motioning for me to shut up. Too late I realize that he might have wanted to play along with the whole Russian angle, just to figure out what she does and doesn't know. But I guess that's lost to us now. Oops. Time to shift to Plan B, I guess. I only hope Tommy has a Plan B.

One thing he does have is an ample inventory of claws, really big claws, and he has them on full display right now, hovering just inches from her nose.

"Ever heard of cat scratch fever, Ms. Strange?" he asks, waving his left paw menacingly in front of her face. I must say, he's got that whole menacing thing down to a science by now.

"What—what do you want from me? How—how did you get inside?" Strange's eyes are darting wildly from side to side, searching for an escape route, and then they suddenly settle on the nightstand. And the missing laptop.

"What—what did you do with my computer?" She starts looking around wildly again, but this time it seems she's worried about something other than making a quick escape. Tommy's smiling devilishly. He clearly knows something about playing with frightened little mice. Just before he kills them and eats them whole. And alive.

"Perhaps I should introduce myself, madam. The name's Tuxedo. Tommy Tuxedo. Agent Double-O Nine, licensed to kill. And if you don't start telling me everything I need to know, I might just have to take full advantage of that license."

Her eyes have stopped moving and are now drilling straight into his. "Double-O? You're from PETSEC—"

"Yes. And right now I'm your very worst nightmare," Tommy growls. "So—the pee-mails—when are the Russians planning on delivering them to you? And when were you planning on releasing them to the general public?"

"I don't have the slightest idea what you're talking about," she answers, indignant. "You two certainly have the nerve, barging in here uninvited, demanding things from me. Stealing my laptop! Why, I have half a mind to—"

"Clearly you have only half a mind, or you never would have gotten mixed up with the Russians in the first place!" Tommy's acting all nonchalant right about now, but he knows as well as I do that a human could prance through the front door any moment now and the jig would be up for us. I decide to help him out.

"Hey, Tommy, now that we've got our hands on her computer, why don't we bug out of here and haul it down to the lab to have Q'ute's people hack into it? I'm sure Ms. Strange here has all kinds of secrets loaded up on that little baby that she'd like to keep to herself. And then meanwhile we can do that little trick you like to use to seal her up in this room tight as a tick, where the humans won't be able to break her out for at least several days." I glance over at the empty Chinese food boxes. "She's got plenty of water in the toilet over there in the bathroom, but she might have to miss a few squares. No big deal, but what dame doesn't want to lose a few extra pounds, anyway?"

I see a twinkle in Tommy's eyes from my mention of his special expertise in sealing up a room. Something that doesn't actually exist, but she doesn't need to know that.

"No! You can't!" Panic is finally starting to settle in with our dear new friend, Julia. "I—there's information on that computer that—they'll kill me if any of that ever gets out!"

Tommy just smiles and starts playing with his claws. "Save me the drama, Strange. You didn't seem to be all that worried about keeping secrets when it was our lives on the line, eh?" He gives me a little side wiggle of his head. "Let's take our stuff and blow this pop stand, Moose. Can't wait to see what she's so all-fired worried about."

Julia is in complete panic mode by now. "No! No, I'll tell you! I'll tell you anything you want to know!"

Tommy considers her through tightly slitted eyes. "Okay, Ms. Strange, I'll give you just one minute to come clean. Twenty questions, okay? Three seconds each." He holds up one claw. "When exactly are you expecting the Russians?"

She's shivering now. Or shuddering. Either way, she's struggling to get out the words. Finally, Tommy makes like he's about to leave, and she breaks down completely, a heaving mess curled up like a doodlebug in the bowels of the recliner. "Stop! They're—I'm supposed to meet them downstairs in the lobby at five o'clock. Precisely. That's when they're supposed to hand over an SD card or thumb drive loaded up with all the pee-mails they downloaded."

"And what were you supposed to do once you got them?" Tommy demands, holding up a second claw.

"I—I'm supposed to hand over all my media contacts and my list of Internet bloggers, all the people I'm releasing the pee-mails to sometime tomorrow afternoon. Just in time to make the late night news cycle."

Tommy is chewing on his lower lip, thinking and mumbling to himself. "Hmm. Five o'clock. That might just give us enough time." He looks up. "Okay, here's the deal. Moose and I will take your laptop with us for insurance. We'll meet up with you down in the lobby just before five with further instructions. You do exactly as I say, and you'll get the laptop back, no questions asked. *Sabe*?"

"I'm sorry, I didn't get that last part," she replies in between generous bursts of tears. "I'm already sobbing, can't you see that?"

"No, I meant—oh, never mind." Tommy motions for me to get ready to bug out. "Just be sure you keep that big snout of yours shut tight, and meet us downstairs on schedule. If you can manage all that, we'll give you back your laptop in one piece. And you might just get out of all of this in one piece yourself."

She nods that she understands what he's asking her to do, then I focus on keeping her distracted while Tommy retrieves the laptop and darts out the door with it, heading straight for the dumbwaiter. As soon as he's clear I give her a short two-finger salute, and then I'm out the door right behind him, racing at full tilt for Q'ute's high tech lab.

Once we're back on the street, Tommy stops for a second to tap on the right side of the weird blue collar Q'ute had given each of us back at the lab.

"Q'ute Branch, Tuxedo here. We've made contact with the Himalayan and are returning to HQ with a special package for your prop heads to tinker with. Meet us there. And I'm going to need you to bring along a couple of extra trinkets if you can…"

Fat Tony's Office, 3:45 p.m.

W hen we finally reach Fat Tony's office, the big cat is nowhere to be found. But an aide from Q'ute Branch is already there waiting for us, and leads us back to the underground lab through a hidden doorway and elevator on the opposite side of the building from the secret entrance where we entered the last time. And I can't tell you how glad I am we don't have to pull that whole plummet into a net thing again. My right leg is still wincing from the last time.

Q'ute is standing just outside the elevator when the doors slide open, looking absolutely stunning in a blue jumpsuit, her Coke bottle glasses and a pair of white cotton gloves. Tommy immediately hands over the small laptop computer we stole from Julia Strange's room.

"We managed to 'borrow' this for a while from that little Himalayan slimeball, Julia Strange, and I'm willing to bet my hind legs it's chock full of secrets we can use to neutralize her going forward. Think your people can figure out a way to clone it before we have to make our way back to the consulate?"

"Not a problem," Q'ute assures him, handling the computer carefully by the edges. "And I'm absolutely delighted to see she chose this particular model. It's quite popular with the 'in' crowd these days, even though it's really pretty pedestrian. But it sports two very interesting features that make it particularly easy to crack."

"Yeah? What's that?" Tommy asks, leaning over to examine the laptop from just inches away.

Q'ute smiles impishly. "Well, for starters, it's secured by a pawprint reader, which users seem to like because it makes it much easier and faster to unlock."

"But we don't actually have one of Strange's paws—" I start to protest.

"No," Q'ute agrees. "But this model also features a beautiful and shiny stainless-steel cover. And unless Mr. Tuxedo managed to smudge the entire surface of the laptop's cover on your way over here, I'm willing to bet—" She holds the computer up at eye level and sideways to the light. "Just as I thought. Several perfectly pristine pawprints, both top and bottom. We should be able to unlock this sweet baby right away, no problem, and simply copy the contents of the disk onto our servers. No decryption needed."

Tommy looks pleased. "And how long will that take? We don't have much time…"

Q'ute hands the computer to her assistant, who drops it carefully into a clear static-free evidence bag. "Don't worry. It shouldn't take more than fifteen to twenty minutes, tops, including the trip to the computer lab and back."

"That'll work out perfectly. Just so long as we leave nothing behind to warn her that she's been compromised, that we're privy to all her secrets. So, one other thing. I called ahead—"

Q'ute stretches out a paw to pat him lightly on the shoulder. "Rest assured, Double-O Nine, my team is already hard at work loading up several USB thumb drives with mock-ups of official PETSEC National Committee emails. And another one that has all the extra features you requested. They'll be ready long before you have to leave for the consulate and the meet-up with the Russian spies."

"Good. Sorry. I'm just a little bit on edge about all of this." Tommy flashes Q'ute what is probably the most conciliatory look I've ever seen from him. Ever.

"No problem, Nine. I think we're all sitting on the edge of the fence top on this right about now. We have very little margin for error in any of this. One little mistake and—"

"We can kiss PETSEC goodbye," Tommy agrees ruefully. "And along with it pretty much the entire planetary feline population. All gone before we can even say meow."

I'm trying to focus on the conversation in front of me, but I can't help but be distracted by a laser beam shining just off to the left that's currently in the business of dissecting a life-size mannequin of a large but otherwise nondescript dog, the beam now slicing through the space immediately north of the mannequin's knees. Tommy's sharp "ahem" brings me back to focus in on the meeting.

Q'ute is quietly laughing at the look that is clearly showing on my face. "Yes, that is one of our more interesting toys, although I'm not exactly sure how we would use it. We have a more portable version, though, that can be used in the field on much smaller animals. Splitting hares, you might say. Very effective at convincing some of your more recalcitrant individuals to spill the beans. One way or another."

I shudder involuntarily at the image, although I have no idea what she means by "recalcitrunk." Must have something to do with math. Division, now that I think about it. Or maybe trees.

Q'ute shows us to a table loaded down with various snacks. "I understand you both missed lunch today, and I wish I had more to offer, but it might be wise to keep up your strength while we still have a few minutes left to kill. And Nine, there's a fresh litter box available through that little door over there, and a fire plug in the corner for you, Moose. Don't want to have to deal with those things in the heat of the moment, you know."

I don't have to be told twice, and dive immediately into a large pile of milky bones before Tommy holds out a paw to stop me.

"Don't overdo it, Moose. You don't want to be slowed down in the middle of a critical undercover stakeout. Plus, we probably need to get you back home before dinnertime, so your humans don't wind up calling out the police to hunt for you."

"Right. Good call." I decide to limit myself to just two milky bones for now. But I stash two more under my collar for later. Just in case.

Q'ute Branch, 4:15 p.m.

I've just finished using the fire plug in the corner when the tech boys arrive with Strange's laptop computer and a silver-colored ziplock bag.

Q'ute is standing with Tommy beside the snack table, talking quietly. The laptop and I arrive at the table almost simultaneously.

"Ah, good. Right on time." Q'ute motions for Tommy to grab the computer but takes the baggie herself. "Getting into the computer was child's play, but there was a ton of interesting stuff stored on the laptop and in her emails, so we'll likely be up all night digging through all of it." She opens the baggie and shakes out three small black squarish-looking thingies.

"Why three?" Tommy asks, taking the baggie as Q'ute dumps them back in.

"One of them has a small red mark on the bottom. That's the special device you requested. Red for Russia, get it?"

Tommy nods yes, and Q'ute continues. "The other two are a standard full-sized SD card, plus a micro SD inserted into a full-size carrier. That way you have two different options on how to handle the switcheroo operation. And unless we get completely screwed and the Russians hand the Himalayan something truly unique and unexpected, like a blue or red card for instance, Strange will never know the difference. But black is a much better color for subterfuge, so I think we're all in safe territory there."

Tommy's wearing some kind of belt pouch around his middle I hadn't noticed before, camouflaged to blend into his fur, and he quickly stashes the little baggie into the pouch, zipping it up securely. The computer he's got tucked under one arm.

"Okay, then," he sighs. "Guess it's now or never. Thanks for all your help, Q'ute. I can't wait to hear what you find out about what other forms of mischief Strange has been up to recently."

"Me neither." Q'ute points to a side door. "You two better get going. I'll have my people escort you out, so you don't get lost. Or accidentally dismembered," she snorts my way. "I take it you remember how to find our main entrance again, once you've completed the drop?"

"I do," Tommy says. "But is there some kind of key—"

"The key is in your collar. It will automatically unlock the portal as you approach it. Just make sure you're not being followed at the time."

"Spycraft 101," Tommy assures her as he hooks a claw over his shoulder toward the door. I get the message. Time for us to hook it.

Ecuadorian Consulate, 4:55 p.m.

O ur brief meet-up with Julia Strange in the lobby went pretty smoothly. She seemed more than relieved to see her laptop still in Tommy's possession, especially after he promised her he would return the computer if she did everything he demanded.

Our stakeout is behind a large potted plant in a dark back corner of the lobby. The Russians are a few minutes late arriving, but considering how hard it is to carry off a casual meet-and-greet between cats and dogs in the middle of a crowded human office building, that was probably to be expected. Plus, they no doubt had to invest quite some time casing the joint for unexpected visitors before ever entering the lobby. Visitors like us.

I'm not sure what I expected a Russian Wolfhound to look like, but this is certainly not it. They just look like a pair of shaggy greyhounds, with mostly whitish fur and several large brownish spots scattered all around for good measure.

"Don't look much like wolves to me," I mumble, mostly to myself.

"Shhh!" Tommy warns me with a hiss, and I shut my trap and burrow deeper into the foliage, still keeping one sharp eye on the Russians and another on the traitorous Julia Strange. An eyeball maneuver that isn't all that easy to pull off, if I must say so myself.

Anyway, one of the Russians is hanging back near the lobby exit, keeping a sharp lookout, while the other one slides smoothly along the bar toward the spot where Strange is standing all alone. They brush past each other very quickly, and then suddenly the Russian is staring back at Strange with concern and confusion spreading across his long face. They exchange a few brief growls, then the Russian seems to have made some kind of decision as he shakes his head once or twice and heads back toward the exit. The whole operation took less than fifteen seconds start to finish, and none of the humans standing around seemed to pay a lick of attention to everything that was happening right at their feet, so to speak.

As soon as the door swung shut on the two Russians and we're in the clear, Tommy is up and across the lobby in a flash, leaving me to saunter more casually across the room, trying to look for all the world like I own the place. Humans will usually defer to a well-bred canine like me if they think I might just belong there. Or, to be exact, belong to someone who belongs there.

By the time I reach them, Tommy is already in the process of handing over the laptop. "Ah-ah-ah," he suddenly tells her, pulling the computer back sharply and handing it to me instead. "First I get to eyeball what they gave you."

Reluctantly, she sticks out a paw, and in the middle of it is one of those little black computer thingies. Tommy snaps it up it instantly and holds it up to the light, shaking his head for a moment before handing it back, then motioning for me to fork over the laptop.

"Satisfied?" Strange asks him with a snarl.

"You just keep that fat nose of yours out of our business from now on, okay, little darlin'?" Tommy snarls back. "No more funny business, or I promise you, our next visit won't be so friendly."

She takes a long hard look at her computer, then slides her eyes back at Tommy, anger and distrust written all over her face. "How do I know you haven't done something—"

"You don't. But, truth be told, you don't have any secrets left that we really care about. Just remember what I said, no more funny business. I don't want to make another house call. The second one seldom works out all that well for my patient."

Grabbing the computer, she turns in a huff and struts off, the laptop clutched under one foreleg and the little black thingie shoved safely underneath her collar. Tommy motions for us to beat a quick retreat outside before the humans finally begin to take notice.

Once outside, though, I turn on him in a huff myself, wanting some quick answers to what I just saw. "That's it? You just give back her the laptop and that black thingie she got from the Russians, simple as that? What about the pee-mails? What about finding out where the Russians are hiding out? We're running out of valuable time, here, Tommy!"

Tommy manages to somehow both smile at me and purse his lips in the process. "Like I said, Moose, you got a lot to learn about being a spy." He motions for me to follow him into a dark hidden-away corner near the Dunkin' Donuts shop before continuing.

"First, Moose, we already dumped the contents of that laptop, so by the time this evening is over we'll have the down and dirty on every single thing she's up to. We'll know, but since she had her laptop locked down with 128-bit encryption, she doesn't know we know, she thinks all of her secrets are still safe. That's a pretty powerful weapon, in and of itself."

I gotta agree with him on that, now that I think about it, but I'm not quite ready to give up the fight just yet. "Okay, then, how about that black computer thingie? I'm pretty sure it's some secret technology the Russians have come up with to stash away all of the stolen pee-mails, and now that she has all of it in her dirty little paws—"

Tommy is rubbing the back of his head with one paw. "Moose, that little black thingie you think might be secret Russian technology is called an SD card. SD stands for Secure Digital, and it's a standard format for a memory card, a way of storing computer data in a very small package. You can buy SD cards pretty much anywhere in the world, right off the shelf."

Okay, he's got me there. But I'm still not giving up that easy. "But, but, you just gave it right back to her. And I'm absolutely convinced it's got all of our secret pee-mails on it. So now she can broadcast them out to the entire world. And that means we're doomed!"

"And that is exactly what we're hoping she'll do. You see, Moose, if you were paying careful attention back at the lab, you'd have noticed that Q'ute handed me some SD cards that looked exactly like the one the Russians gave her, the one with all our pee-mails on it. When I took the Russian SD card from her and pretended to take a long hard look at it, I secretly switched the Russian card for an almost identical card from Q'ute. A card that was loaded to the gills with fake pee-mails that make Fat Tony and the entire PETSEC organization seem like a bunch of bear cub scouts, totally sweet and innocent. If she does decide to release them—which we're betting she'll do without even looking at them, trusting that the Russians have handed her something very juicy and damning to our side—that will only make us all look like perfect little angels. And if the Russians ever try to release the real pee-mails later on, Strange's version will give us cover to insist that the Russian version is all fake news."

Tommy's right, maybe I really am way too stupid to be a secret agent, after all. He and Q'ute are operating at a level way above my kibble grade. But—

"Okay, I get it, pretty clever really, but there's still that thing about the Russian base of operations. How can we possibly track them down now? We have no idea even which way they turned when they left the consulate building."

Tommy has that weird smile/pursed lips thing going on again. "You're right, Moose. Maybe I should have hidden out inside the lobby and watched the swap take place while you sat out here and tailed the Russians to their secret lair. And that might have worked, assuming two of Russia's best-trained and most ruthless operatives could somehow be tracked by a lap dog Yorkie from the suburbs without them turning on him in some dark alley and gutting him like a fish before he could even get out a single bark. But what Q'ute and I decided on, instead, was for Strange to hand them an SD card of her own, one that holds very little in the way of data but does hold a microminiature transmitter. A transmitter that they are now carrying straight back to their secret lair and a certain evil mastermind named Vladimir Kitin. So, what do you think now about our little Plan B option?"

Ordinarily I would be right in his face about that snarky little Yorkie reference, but right about now

I don't feel like I could take on a wounded butterfly. Much less a master spy who really does deserve the whole Double-O status. Licensed to kill, and right now my own ego is ready to be buried alive. If it had any life left, that is. Weakly, I manage to get in one last word on the subject. And even that's just a surrender. "Okay. That makes sense, I guess. Good idea. So, what do we do next?"

"*We* do nothing, Moose. I've still got a long night ahead of me, working with the lab rats to locate the Russian HQ and draw up a plan for putting a stop to whatever nefarious plans they've put in place for screwing up the election."

"So, okay, where does that leave me?" I ask in a tellingly squeaky voice.

"I think you've done enough—" He hesitates for a moment, and I can almost hear the word he's decided to leave out. *Damage*. "—for one day. Like I said before, you had best head home before your humans panic and get the police, the firefighters and half of the armed forces out on the streets hunting you down. Get some dinner and a good night's rest. If you still feel up to it, meet me at the lab early tomorrow morning. Your collar will let you in."

Oh. That reminds me. When they swapped out my collar for this funny little blue thingie, will it still work my doggie door? And what if my humans notice the switch? I can't exactly show up scratching on the back door begging to be let in, they'll notice it in a heartbeat. So I have a lot to worry about as I turn and start trotting my way back home, my head hung low. I've got a lot to think about, for sure.

Home, 5:45 p.m.

I got lucky with the trains, and also lucky with the collar. Q'ute must've had them stick something in it to trigger my doggie door because it worked without a hitch, and my humans already had my food bowl laid out on the floor waiting for me.

My head is still buzzing from all the events of the day, and no matter how hard I try, I can't seem to think of anything I really added to the effort, except maybe distracting Julia Strange while Tommy took off with her laptop. He really had the whole thing under control, start to finish. Maybe tomorrow I'll just be better off staying home and leaving all the spy work to the pros.

A sharp bark from outside, somewhere out back, stirs me from my troubled thoughts, and I trot slowly toward the back door to check it out. Once I'm down the steps I glance off to my left and see immediately I was right—the bark was from Bella, the Corgi who lives next door. My girlfriend. Or, more realistically, just my girl friend. Of all the dogs in the entire universe, she has the least delusions about my particular role in this world. She's got my complete measure. And it isn't very long.

"Moose!" She's sitting at the fence, and I notice right away that her ears are drooping, and her tail is lying flat. "Where have you been? I've been sitting here barking for hours!"

That's not exactly new news. Even more so than most Corgis, Bella has a real yapper on her. A nonstop yapper. I think she might even bark in her sleep.

"Hey, Bella. Sorry, I got called downtown. An emergency down at PETSEC." I decide to not dive into any of the details. Bella has told me in no uncertain terms my hero days are long behind me. And, after today, I'm beginning to think she's completely right on that score. Besides, she's wearing a real hangdog look I've never seen on her before, so I sure don't want to add to her troubles. I decide to change the subject. "What's going on, B? You seem sad. Is everything okay? How did the doctor visit go?"

I can see her big brown eyes starting to fill up with fat tears, spilling over and trickling down her muzzle, something I've never seen her do before. And somehow it seems to be catching. "No, Moose," she blurts out in a leaden voice. "Everything is not okay. Everything is really bad, as a matter of fact. Really, really bad."

The tears are already falling in a steady stream as I shove my nose through the chain link fence for a gentle bump. "Did someone get hurt?" I seem to recall her human mistress acting a little off recently, and sounds coming from inside of Bella's house like the ones I make when I eat too fast and toss it all back up. Which isn't all that bad, really, once you get through all the retching. It's like getting two meals for the price of one.

But I suddenly realize Bella's been talking all the while I've been thinking. Which is my usual go-to move, given she rattles on pretty much nonstop, but right now I think she might actually have something important to say.

"—so it seems my humans are getting a little baby human pretty soon, a human puppy, and I heard them talking about maybe giving me away—"

"Giving you away!" I can't believe what I just heard! Bella's humans? Talking about engaging in canine trafficking? That can't be true! That's just so— inhuman! "But Bella, surely you must have misunderstood them. I mean, the way humans garble all their words and such, it's pretty much impossible to really follow along when they—"

"No, Moose, I know what I heard. They're serious about it. It seems they've been worried for a long time about all my barking—"

"They can't restrict your First Amendment rights! There's nothing wrong with your barking, you just have a lot more to say than most dogs. We'll sue!"

"Yeah, well, good luck with that." Bella glances back toward her house. "But, the problem is, my mistress thinks the noises I make will wind up disturbing the new puppy when it comes. She says it's already disturbing her, and the puppy isn't even here yet. And—and my master agrees."

"But—but—you were here first! After all, this is your home as much as it is theirs. If your barking presents a problem for their new human puppy, then—they'll just have to cancel it, is all. Squatters rights. And you are a squatter, after all. You know, being that you're a girl —"

"I don't think it's that easy, Moose. I know you've never been around a human puppy—except for that one time, and the humans seem to have made a concerted effort to keep them away from you ever since—but the humans are really weird about their puppies. Remember Angie down the street? It wasn't long after the first human puppy arrived in her house that they built her a doghouse and banished her to the backyard pretty much full time."

"But they didn't try to sell her off into dog slavery!" Even the thought of that had my dinner already threating to visit me again. And I know what I said earlier about twice being nice, but this time I don't think I could force myself to get it back down my throat again. "I remember when we were trying to locate a good home for Killer, after everyone got sprung out of prison, and some of the stories I heard about how some humans treat their dogs were just—sickening!"

"Nevertheless, Moose, it is what it is. If they decide to sell me off to the highest bidder—the word they like to use is 'adopt', like it somehow makes it all acceptable—then I don't really have any say in the matter, do I?" The tears were still falling in a steady flow, forming a small puddle at her feet. Which are huge, by the way, given how short her legs are. "It's all kind of funny in a way, you know, Moose? Because having a say in the matter is really why I'm in this whole mess in the first place. I can't seem to just shut up."

I was just about to suggest that solution to her, but now I realize it wouldn't have helped the situation at all, given the circumstances. Bella is who she is, and Corgis are no more capable of being shy, quiet shrinking violets than I am of turning down a chewstick. If a butterfly flaps its wings in Brazil, those Corgi ears of hers are going to hear it, and then she just can't help but let everyone in the whole wide world know about it. A regular chatterbox.

And I'm pretty much the opposite of all that. I struggle to say anything at all, and even then it usually comes out all wrong, somehow. Like right now—I know I should be saying something to comfort her, but for the life of me I don't have a clue what that might be. She just seems so pathetic, standing there with her whole life draining from her eyes... and suddenly it hits me. If Bella leaves, then I'll have lost my bestest friend in the whole world, for the second time this year. First Killer, then Bella, and then who do I got left to hang out with? Who do I got left to talk to?

As the reality of all that finally sinks in, Bella suddenly starts getting all blurry in my eyes. I reach out a paw to grab the fence and steady myself, even as a strange, raw emptiness bursts open from somewhere way deep within my chest, tearing away at me. Everything around me starts to spin, and I just can't help myself, I throw back my head in pain. And howl.

Home, 7:30 p.m.

My humans have just finished their din-din, but instead of watching television until bedtime like every other night, they're standing in the living room, arguing. Something I've never really seen them do before. I'd snuck Bella in through the doggie door a little earlier so we could talk some more, since the night was getting too cold to stay outside, and now we're hunkered down together under the dining room table, listening in.

My mistress, Helen, is speaking in a very loud voice, her words sounding like what you might expect a toy poodle to sound like if it was human. Squeaky, high pitched, but soothing in its own unique way. Howard, on the other hand, has a slightly nasally voice. Which is odd, really, given how short his nose really is. Back to Helen.

"Oh my stars! I never in my entire life expected to hear those words come out of your mouth, Howard McGillicutty!"

"Now, Helen—"

"Don't you now Helen me! Of all the harebrained ideas—"

"I'm not trying to reach any conclusions about any of this tonight, I'm just saying we might want to consider—"

"Consider getting rid of Moose? Really?"

That certainly got my attention. I mean, it's usually pretty hard to follow humans when they're talking. Unlike animals, they're known for having exceedingly poor enunciation, and half their words sound like a great many other completely different words, so it's important to stay focused on context. But "getting rid of Moose"? That came through loud and clear.

"Listen, Helen, just think about what this all means to us. All of us, even Moose. I'm just saying the Pattersons might have the right idea, after all. Sometimes finding a new home for the dog might be the best thing for *him*, as well. Take the stress off of everyone, the dog included. I mean, you heard the howling last night. He's clearly not happy here."

"No, you mean take the stress off of *you*, is what I'm hearing! You couldn't care less about the dog. You never have. It's always about you, isn't it? It's always about your job, your career, what *you* need, and I'm always just supposed to go along with all of it.

'Oh, yes, Helen. I got a new job in London, and we're moving in a few weeks. So you need to sell the house, pack up our things, quit your job, and say goodbye to all of your friends. And, oh, by the way, get rid of the dog while you're at it.' Does that sound about right? Because that's exactly how I heard it!"

Helen is darting jerkily around the room, dusting everything she comes across, something she always does when she's angry. Which means this room rarely ever gets dusted. But it's getting the grand treatment tonight, that's for sure.

"Look, Helen, I think you're being a little unfair, here—"

"Unfair? You think *I'm* being unfair? Is that what you think? Well let me tell you something about fairness, mister. When you first asked me to marry you, you promised me I would always have an equal say in our marriage, that I would never be forced to take a back seat to your life, your career. But how exactly has that worked out, huh? You moved me out here to Chicago from the wonderful, comfortable world I had built for myself, for *us*, in Cincinnati. My family, my friends, my job. My career. But it was a great opportunity for you, the chance of a lifetime, the best thing for the both of us, you said. And I went along with it. I mean, what else was I supposed to do? Divorce you? No, I did the dutiful wifely thing, I stuck by my man, moved out here where I knew not a single solitary soul, and tried to start my life up all over again."

"But Helen, at the time we thought maybe you could stay home—"

I'm not really following any of this, but whatever he just said really must have set her off, because she started bawling just like Bella did earlier tonight.

"Thank you for reminding me about that! Thank you for reminding me that I'm *sterile*, that I can never have children. You have no idea what I would do to be pregnant like Susan. No idea!"

"Helen, what I meant was—"

"No, I know what you meant. I know exactly what you meant."

"Listen—"

"No, I'm tired of listening to you. You need to listen to me for a change. I can't have children. I know that, and I accept that. I have to, I have no other choice in the matter. But with you gone all the time, traveling,

Moose is the only comfort I have around this house. I can't have children, but I can have him. And you are *not* going to take him away from me!"

That part I got, and I'm starting to breathe a little easier right about now. But still—if Bella leaves the neighborhood, where will that leave me? Maybe I just need to think this one through a little better...

My master has managed to get in front of Helen and is holding her by the shoulders. And she's refusing to look his way, her tears still pouring out down her face. "But—Helen. Let's be reasonable. Please. You know, honey, when we get to London, we'll have the entire continent of Europe at our doorstep. You'll want to be traveling all the time, to Paris, Rome, Athens. A dog would just be an anchor to us. And on a boat—"

"Yes, and that whole boat thing is your idea, mister, not mine. You think *I* want to live on a barge in the middle of the Thames River like some kind of vagabond? All because we can't afford anything else closer in to the city, and you refuse to commute to work like everybody else? And don't even try to talk to me about traveling. I've heard that particular tune before, a thousand times over, already. And just who winds up doing the traveling while I stay behind and keep everything neat and tidy for when you finally decide to drag yourself home like some conquering hero? No, I know exactly how London will turn out. I'll be all alone once again, stuck on a cold, leaky barge, with no family, no friends. I can't get a *job* in England because I'm just the spouse of a person who *can* get a work visa. And my family will be a ten or fifteen hour plane ride away, even if any of them could even afford the fare. I guess I should just drop down on my knees and thank you for taking me someplace where they at least speak English! Thank you, my dear husband. I am so blessed to serve you. Truly."

My master looks like he's run out of steam. Or at least out of arguments. But he seems to still have one last card to play, hidden up his sleeve.

"Helen, we don't even know if we *can* bring Moose to England. The last I heard, we'd have to stick him in some kind of quarantine cage for six months or a year—"

"Well, unlike you, *Howard*, I've checked into that. When England joined the EU they had to change a lot of their rules, and one of them was the quarantine issue. The EU had a rule that animals could travel freely within the Union as long as they had a veterinary certificate proving they were fully vaccinated against rabies and all of the other serious diseases. And as it turns out, our vet is fully certified to sign off on one of those. So Moose is every bit as welcome in jolly old England as you and I are. Plus, British Air will let him travel with us in the main cabin, one of the advantages of having a smaller dog. So there. Either he goes with us, or I stay! You want to be the decider, here? Then decide!"

"You can't be serious, Helen. Choosing a dog over—"

"I'm not choosing anything, Howard. It's not my choice, it never has been. I'm perfectly content staying right here, continuing the life that I've finally built for myself here in Chicago, such as it is. It's you that wants to stir things up, it's you that's forcing everything to change. All so you can get a fancy new job. Okay, then, go. Have fun. But I'm tired of always taking the back seat in our marriage. I'm ready to call my own shots for a change. And that all starts with Moose. At least he's loyal. At least he loves me. I'm not sure I can say the same about you."

"Oh, Helen, of course I—"

But he doesn't get to finish the sentence, because my mistress Helen has stormed into the bedroom and slammed the door. I signal to Bella and we sneak out of the dining room as quietly as we can, while Howard stands all by himself in the living room and fumes.

Fat Tony's Office,
Early Monday Morning

A fter breakfast I stepped outside to check on how Bella was getting along, but as soon as she saw me she burst into tears again and bolted for the inside. After all my howling last night, I can't say I blame her.

Inside the house, the mood was scarcely any better. Last night's argument was clearly still bothering Helen, my mistress. But not half as much as it was bothering me. First Bella, now me, sold into canine slavery like we were common barnyard animals? How could my world get any more upside down than this?

And as if things couldn't get any worse, my mistress was now crashing around the house, busily packing away various things she'd pulled off of shelves and out of drawers into little brown cardboard boxes, cursing under her breath the whole time. Something about watching my humans packing stuff up really bothers me for some reason I can't explain, so I figure I'll be much happier checking out the action at PETSEC HQ instead. Find out what if anything they had located on Julia Strange's computer.

When I get to Fat Tony's office, there are well over a dozen people packed into the room, moving back and forth seemingly at random, and I have to step back for a moment to take it all in. I'm about to decide that I should just take off and head back home, when out of nowhere someone grabs my shoulder from behind.

"Moose! I thought you'd fallen off the face of the earth. I already put out word on the squirrel network, asking Sammy to find you and haul your hairy butt down here. We need you!"

It's Fat Tony, in the flesh. Well, what flesh he has left, after losing all that weight.

"Hey, Tony. Sorry. Some problems at home I needed to take care of this morning." I tilt my head toward all the hustle and bustle in the office. "What's up?"

Tony's smile was so wide it could probably light up the room all on its own. "Well, to start with, Moose, that bait-and-switch caper you pulled off with Tommy yesterday worked like a charm. Julia Strange dumped the contents of the fake SD card onto the

Internet without ever once checking to see what was on it, and now all the news shows and pet blogs are lighting up with how progressive PETSEC and its leadership really is. Especially toward feline empowerment. We may have just turned the tide on the whole election!"

"Hey, that's great news!" And obviously, from Tony's perspective, it really is. If the detective business has really been as bad as he makes out, he really needs a steady job right about now, and they don't get any cushier than president of PETSEC. "So, are we done then?" I wag my head in the direction of all the people racing madly around us. "What's with all the activity all of a sudden?"

Tony managed to smile even wider. "The bug Q'ute stuck in the fake SD card paid off big time. We know where the Russians have holed up in the city, and now Tommy is organizing a raid on their headquarters to put them away for good. Before they can stir up any more trouble around here."

I can't help but swallow an involuntary lump in my throat at that news. "A—raid? That sounds— dangerous. But hey, I'm happy to help out any way I can. Maybe I can hang back here and help man the radios…"

"No way I'd ask that of you, Moose," Tony exclaims, slapping me harshly and unexpectedly between my shoulder blades. "No, you and Tommy are the real heroes, here, so you deserve to be in the thick of the action when we take them all down! Without everything you two pulled off yesterday, we'd probably all be packing up the office and writing my concession speech right about now!"

Just at that moment I see Tommy heading our way, the crowd parting ever so slightly to give him room.

"Moose! Glad you could finally join us! Have a little too much late night fun last night? Morning come way too early for ya?"

I bump paws with Tommy as he finally works his way through the mayhem. "No, just had some things pop up with the day job I needed to handle before I headed on over." No way I was going to spill the kibble on what was really going on back home. Some things are just too personal, if you know what I mean.

Tommy twitches his tail knowingly. "Gotcha. Yeah, I know how it is. Even with all the useless leeches I've got hanging around on my payroll, sometimes a problem pops up that just needs *el jefe* to weigh in and take command of the situation." He raised an eyebrow in Tony's direction. "You catch him up on what's been happening around these parts while he's been catching up on his beauty sleep?"

"Some of it. I was just getting to the part about the raid on the tearoom."

Tearoom? Suddenly the raid didn't seem all that scary, after all. I mean, how scary could a bunch of old ladies sitting around sipping tea and eating finger sandwiches really be?

Tommy twitches again, this time in my direction. "Good. Then it's all set. We'll hit the tearoom HQ inside the hour. I'll take the lead with the commando team, and Moose can cover the rearguard action, just in case any loose ends try to slip past my little dragnet."

Rearguard? This is starting to sound better and better. "Just point me in the right direction, then, and I'll get it done. Loose ends are my specialty." That didn't exactly come out the way I intended, but no one seemed to notice. Or at least no one decided to comment on it. And for Tommy, that was a major improvement from the day before. Maybe he didn't see me as such a big loser after all.

Tommy appears distracted, and glances briefly over my shoulder at someone, then holds up a paw, a single claw poking out of it. "Super. Okay, then, we meet outside in five, and go from there. You need to step into the little girl's room in the meantime?" he asks, staring pointedly at me with a small smirk showing on his face. Maybe I was too quick to judge the change in our relationship, after all. But no way I was going to let my irritation show.

"Nah, I'll save it all up to mark up the tearoom nice and smelly when we're done. Cover up anything those Wolfhounds have left behind so there won't be any record left that they had ever set paw in there."

"Good thinking, Moose," Tony says, giving me another unexpected slap on my back, as Tommy somehow manages to melt away back into the crowd. "But don't forget, your stuff isn't encrypted, so watch what you say, right?"

"Don't worry, Tony," I promise him with a tellingly serious look. "I think we've all learned our lesson about that!"

Russian Tearoom

Our objective is laid out straight across the street from us. All in all, it doesn't look all that imposing, just a glass-fronted restaurant, like pretty much any other restaurant in downtown Chicago. Which I guess is pretty much the point— what use is a secret headquarters, after all, if the place screams Secret Headquarters just by looking at it?

Tommy had sent one group of commandos into the alley around back to seal off the rear exits, and two other teams are positioned off to the left and right to execute what Tommy called a "pincher" movement, whatever that is. My job is to maintain my observation point behind a large mailbox while the rest of the team dashes across the street and into the tearoom. The element of surprise is key here. Any advance warning that we are coming could have very dire consequences. Very dire, indeed.

As the team leaders flanking the front entrance signal they're ready, Tommy checks for cars, then holds up one paw for a second before bringing it down sharply and racing across the street, with his attack team in hot pursuit. Almost immediately they are dashing through the front door, with the rest of the commandos moving to cover the entrance, and instantly earsplitting screams start to erupt from inside the small restaurant. I desperately want to know what is going down inside, whether our team had gotten themselves caught in some kind of ambush and were being sliced up by the Russians, but Tommy had made my duty crystal clear. Hold down the mailbox at any cost.

In the end, it was all over in less than a minute. Almost the very same moment Tommy and his team had rushed the front door, humans began to shove their way free of the small tearoom like their butts were on fire, screaming and pointing and racing in every direction at once. It was all I could do to sort through the whole madhouse scene to make sure none of the Russian Wolfhounds were trying to take advantage of the craziness to somehow try and slip past me. But that wasn't going to happen, not with me on the job!

Anyway, almost before the raid started, it's over, and Tommy is throwing open the front door of the joint and stepping out into the light with a deep scowl plastered on his face, his tail tucked tight against his legs. I know without asking that something had gone terribly wrong with the raid. Terribly wrong, indeed.

Fat Tony's Office

We are all gathered around the conference table back at PETSEC's temporary new headquarters to debrief on what Tommy had learned from the aborted raid.

Tony can't believe what he was hearing. "Nothing? You got nothing? How is that even possible?"

That would have been the first question out of my mouth, if I'd been running the debrief. We had top-notch intel placing the Russians inside the tearoom, but when the raiding party blasted inside, there was no trace of them whatsoever. Just a terrified handful of humans, who had up till then been peacefully enjoying tiny little pots of tea before all heck broke loose inside the restaurant.

Tommy is scowling down at the table in front of him. "It isn't. I mean, our intel from the transmitter was unimpeachable. The Russians left the meet-and-greet with Julia Strange and went straight to the tearoom. Q'ute assures me there was no mistake about that. But when we executed the raid, when we got inside the place, there was no sign whatsoever that the

Wolfhounds had ever been there. And believe me, we checked. We checked behind every door, pulled up every rug, turned over every speck of dust. But we found nothing. Nada. By the time the human cops showed up we had all but pulled up the floorboards in the place. But not one single hint that the Russians had ever been there."

"But—but that's impossible!" I've never seen Tony red-faced before, but now it looks like he might be ready to explode right in front of us. "The only way they could have possibly known we were raiding the place is—"

"We have a mole inside of PETSEC," Tommy finished for him.

The news about a mole inside of PETSEC hit the room like that Churnable nucular plant Q'ute told us about yesterday. The one that got to Vladimir Kitin and his family.

"A mole?" Tony's face has somehow managed to get even redder than before, if that was even possible. "How can that be? We got no moles in

156

PETSEC. I—I don't even know if I'd recognize one if I saw it!"

"Well, on the surface they look kinda like a particularly ugly form of mouse or rat," some aide suggests from the back of the room. "Except they're mostly pretty blind, and hide out underground for almost their entire lives, where their diet consists almost exclusively of earthworms. But I can't imagine why they'd be at all interested in PETSEC's presidential election..."

Tommy is shaking his head, fully irritated now. "No, no, not an actual mole, you fools. I'm talking about a spy. A spook. Somebody the Russians have planted inside our organization to keep tabs on what we're up to. That's the only way they could have known about the raid in time to bug out of the tearoom before we got there."

"It makes sense..." Tony's chewing on his lower lip now, lost in thought. "And that could also explain how they figured out how to decrypt all the pee-mails. A spy inside of Q'ute's organization..."

Tommy's face looks like it could kill something all on its own. "Which means they probably have access to all of the other high-tech gear Q'ute

Branch has been putting together for us. Once again, the Russians don't have the actual smarts to create any of that state-of-the-art technology, but they're more than capable of stealing it from us and copying it all at will."

The table got quiet for a moment, and I took that as my cue to butt in. "All of this is very interesting, but what the heck do we do about it? If there's a spy working for Q'ute, how can we possibly hunt him down before the election? And if the Russians are still running around Chicago free and clear, how do we keep them from causing even more mischief? We're running out of time on this, folks!"

Tommy's face seems to clear a bit as he stares up at me, catching my eye. "Moose is right. As bad as this new bit of info is, we don't have time to deal with it directly right now. We have an election to save, and if we screw up that particular mission, mole or no mole, it just won't matter anymore. So, any thoughts?

I clear my throat slightly to get everyone's attention. "Uh, Tommy? Tony? Given the situation here, don't you guys think we should break up this meeting and huddle up together in an executing session?"

Tommy manages to smile at that, although I don't really know why. "Executive session? Actually, Moose, that is a splendid suggestion. I should have thought of that myself." He sticks his left paw out and waves it around the table. "Okay, everybody, back to your day jobs for now. Let's clear out the room. Moose, Tony, the three of us need to talk in private."

Tony's head is slowly nodding as he works through all the detailed implications of Tommy's plan. "So right, I agree, we can all assume Q'ute herself isn't the mole. But everyone directly below her is fully suspect, so we can't trust any of them. And that goes for my staff as well."

"And my own staff inside my company," Tommy adds. "In fact, other than the three of us—and Q'ute, of course—we have to assume everyone inside of PETSEC is a potential undercover agent for the Russians. And the Crimson Canines, for that matter."

"But we need to keep that fact to ourselves," I suggest conspiratorially. "I mean, that cat is already out of the bag, so to speak, after the mostly public debrief meeting, but surely we can do something to keep that information from spreading throughout the entire organization."

Tony smiles back at me grimly, his canines flashing. "I'll issue orders right away that if anyone says one word about having a spy among us, I'll personally tie him inside a big canvas bag and throw his sorry butt into the Chicago River. That should do the trick."

"Good." Tommy is wearing a look like he's done with all the talking and is ready to once again take command of the situation. "So we've got our assignments. Tony, you hold down the fort here. Moose and I, we have some field work to take care of. If there's one thing we proved in spades in dealing with Julia Strange—there's more than one way to skin a rat. Or, in this case, a mole."

Q'ute Branch, Noon

We're all huddled in a tiny room buried deep in the back of Q'ute's top-secret laboratories, dozens of floors beneath the busy streets of the Miracle Mile. Q'ute quietly double-checks the locks on the door, then flips a small red switch mounted on the wall right next to the door.

"This room is equipped with a SCIF, so anything we say will be kept completely confidential," Q'ute explains, pointing to the switch.

"A Sniff?" I ask, completely perplexed. "You mean there's like a big giant nose sucking all the air out of the room? That sounds pretty dangerous!"

Not for the first time, Tommy shakes his head at me. "No, Moose, not a sniff. A SCIF. We're inside a Sensitive Compartmented Information Facility, filled with various electronic countermeasures to confuse any bugs that might be planted on us, or anyone trying to listen in from the outside."

"Uh, I knew that," I suggest. "Just trying to keep things light here…"

Tommy's twitching whiskers are saying he isn't buying it. Not one bit. "Right. Okay, then, let's get down to business, shall we? By the way, thanks for setting this up at the last minute, Q'ute. It's important that we talk to you in private. We—we think you may have a mole planted somewhere inside of Q'ute Branch."

Q'ute's eyes widen with alarm. "A mole? Oh my gosh! That's impossible! I've personally vetted every single animal who works for me. In fact, I microchipped them myself. There's no way—"

"And yet apparently there is," Tommy interrupts. "Someone leaked the raid on the Russian tearoom, and when we got there, the whole place was clean as a cat's paw. No sign of the Russians anywhere."

"But that could have come from your team—"

"Not a chance. Tony and Moose were the only members of the team other than me who were informed about our target in advance. And I think you'll agree they are both totally trustworthy."

Q'ute eyes me kinda funny for a long moment, but finally shakes her head. "Okay, that makes sense, I guess. Although I really wish you were wrong about all this. The work we're doing down here, it's all extremely sensitive—"

"And now I think you can count on almost all of it being the property of SPECTER at this point. And probably at some point the entire Russian Government."

"Which means that once we find the spy, we'll have to chuck the whole shooting match down the chute and start working on creating new countermeasures for our own weapons. What fun."

Q'ute is looking anything but happy right now, so I decide to try and cheer her up.

"Hey, the good news is, these high tech collars of yours really work! I especially like the way you put a little doodad in mine to open up my electronic doggie door!"

"Doggie door?" Q'ute mutters, still somewhat dazed. "No, we didn't—"

Tommy leans in over the table, tapping the center of it with one paw for emphasis. "Our first order of business here is to find some way to neutralize the spy, and Fat Tony has a few interesting ideas along those lines. You know how that works, if you want to catch a thief, you gotta start by thinking like a thief, and if you want to catch a two-timing fink, well..."

I think that was intended as some kind of snide remark about Tony, which I think is kinda out of order right now. I mean, we're all on the same team, here, so we gotta stick together until we see this whole thing through. I'm just about to say so when I realize Q'ute and Tommy have been discussing the details of the plan, so I lean in myself to try and catch up.

"...feed the spook some disinformation, to keep the Russians unsteady on their paws, get them watching left while we come at them from the right," Tommy's saying.

"Ah, the old double-triple-cross," Q'ute notes with a sly smirk. "I like it, Tommy. Great idea. And meanwhile I can activate a little sniffer program on our primary communications conduits to see if we can trace the message back to the sender. Catch our little mole pink-handed, as it were."

Aha! I knew my sniffer suggestion would come in handy at some point! I was just a little ahead of my time, I guess.

"Then we're all set." Tommy hops up and makes like he's getting ready to leave. "You know what we're up to over the next few hours, so I'll leave it to you to concoct a believable lie and feed it to the mole. And Q'ute—" He gives her a very serious face. "We're running out of time, here. Every minute is precious if we're going to save this election and run the Russians out of town for good."

"I hear you," Q'ute answers, raising her ears just slightly to make her point. "I'll have everything in place within thirty minutes. I could make it faster, but I don't want to draw attention—"

"To the fact that we just had this secret meeting. Gotcha. Okay, thirty minutes it is. That'll give Moose and I just enough time to get back to our temporary HQ and set everything in motion. And, Q'ute—thanks."

"No need to thank me. If I hadn't been so lax with security around here in the first place, you'd already have Vladimir Kitin and his goons locked up and headed back to Russia. Now I've just got to make it right. And hope that we've caught wind of this mole of mine in time to keep Boss Dawg from getting elected." A shiver seems to run through her for a moment, then she runs her paws down the front of her lab coat, straightening it where it didn't need to be straightened, and points toward the door. "You two should go first, so we're not seen walking out of here

165

together. I'll hang back a few minutes longer and compose my false flag message."

"Good idea." Tommy nods at me, and we quickly unlock the door and find our way slowly to the elevator and out of the underground lab, making sure the entire time we aren't being watched by the mole or any of his friends. The elevator ride to the top is strangely quiet as we both ponder what strange and dangerous developments lay ahead of us over the next few hours.

Ecuadorian Consulate, 12:45 p.m.

S peaking of strange, on our way back to HQ Tommy suddenly got a wild hair to check up on our old friend from Kitty-Leaks, Julia. The Ecuadorian Consulate wasn't very far out of our way, and he thought it might be a good idea to warn her that the Russians were still in the city. And that they might not be all that happy with her right about now.

As we turn the corner a few blocks down from the embassy, we can't help but notice that the entire street seems to be filled up with police cars and ambulances. A mob of onlookers had formed, as they always do, so it takes quite an effort for Tommy and me to squeeze past all of the legs and feet to find out what had happened.

As we get to the front, a group of humans, mostly coppers, are all standing in a circle around something that had been covered up by a sheet. By the size and shape of it, I am pretty sure we were looking down at all that was left of Julia Strange.

"No one saw it happen, but it appears she must have jumped from that window up there," one of the coppers is saying, pointing a pencil toward an open window on the fourth floor.

"What in the world would cause a cat like that to want to commit suicide?" another copper asks. "And why the heck didn't it land on its feet?"

"Don't know," the first copper answers, pausing to write something into a small notepad. "And she ain't got no collar, so there's no ID on her. I put word out inside the building, but nobody's claiming ownership of her. I guess we can write this one up to just another unsolved mystery. This city's full of 'em."

Tommy motions for me to fall back, so we quickly turn and head left, toward Fat Tony's office. When we finally make our way free of the crowd, he pulls me aside into a small break between two buildings.

"Guess we were too late, Moose. The Russians clearly got to her before we could. Probably steaming mad about what got released to the press." He pauses a second to look back. "Our little bait-and-switch with the fake SD card turned out to be a killer idea after all, even if it didn't lead us to the Russians."

I wince a little at his pun. Too soon, I guess. But that got me to thinking. "Whatever happened to the little thingie with the secret transmitter?" I ask him.

"We found it inside the tearoom, near the back, out by the alley entrance. They obviously left it there to lure us in. I'm just surprised they didn't plan an ambush for us when we finally showed up."

"That suggests they didn't have a lot of time, doesn't it? That they had to bug out of the restaurant at the last moment? That might be useful information for Q'ute as she tries to track down the spy inside her lab."

"Great idea, Moose! Don't know why I didn't think of it earlier. I'll send Q'ute a secure message over the collarphone to let her know—"

Tommy gets busy for almost a minute tapping something out on his collar, then gazes up at me, one eyebrow cocked. "Q'ute says she already has a hot lead for us."

"Already? It hasn't even been thirty minutes yet—"

"No, not from the false flag message. She got a note from someone deep inside the Russian organization. A dame. Says she's heard of your reputation and wants to meet up with us to hand over some files she's managed to smuggle out of SPECTER. This could be the big break we've been looking for!"

"I don't know, Tommy. It all seems a little— convenient, don't you think? It might be a trap."

"Yeah, Q'ute thinks so, too. But at this point, even walking into a trap might somehow lead us to SPECTER and help us crack this thing. So I guess we just gotta go into it with both eyes wide open. And keep a sharp lookout for any tasty morsels of cheese that are laid out suspiciously in broad daylight, just waiting to lure us in."

"Okay, sounds like a plan. Although me and cheese don't do all that well together. Lactose intolerant, you know. But alright, what are we waiting for then? Let's hit it. Where did Q'ute suggest we should meet up?"

"At the Shedd Aquarium. There's a new exhibit there that hasn't yet been opened up to the general public. Q'ute's sending over the GPS coordinates right as we speak."

Almost as soon as he said the words, Tommy's collar pings, and the collar starts talking to us in a squeaky, high-pitched voice, in a tone way out of range of human hearing, handicapped as they are.

"Turn left, stay on the sidewalk for two blocks…"

Shedd Aquarium, 1:30 p.m.

E ven though the aquarium isn't all that far away as the crow flies, it seems like forever on my four little paws, especially since I've already gotten in more walkies today than I usually get in a week. On a good week when it isn't raining. And I can't help but notice that my breakfast from earlier this morning is already starting to wear a bit thin.

Tommy's collar has us sneaking into the aquarium through a loading dock, then up some stairs to what appears to be the top floor. Some yellow tape is stretched between the stair rails on either side of us, blocking off the top of the stairs, but we slip easily underneath it and make our way down a short hallway to a nondescript set of double doors blocking the entrance to the building. Tommy and I have stopped to consider exactly how we are ever going to get the doors open, when all of a sudden a high-pitched voice—not from Tommy's collar, but from a speaker mounted overhead—announces 'Enter' and the doors slowly swing open. With one quick glance at each other, Tommy and I hurry inside. I get a brief whiff of some kind of cheese coming from the other side of the doorway, but it might just be my imagination.

The room we walk into is all stark white, and completely empty except for one other door set into the opposite wall. We've only made it a few feet into the room when I hear a sudden noise behind us and spin around just in time to see the double doors slam shut with a loud *CLICK*, a sound that echoes off the blank white walls in the room, making it crystal clear we are now trapped like two little mice in a cage. I try the handle on the door, but no matter how hard I pull on it, the handle refuses to budge. And, not meaning to brag or anything, but I gotta lot of muscle on me for a ten pound dog, so it's clear the door is securely locked. "Maybe we should try the other door?" I suggest.

No sooner had I voiced that thought than the other door slowly opened, and a tall, furry white dog stepped through. Her eyes were a deep shade of blue, and almost almond in shape.

"Samoyed," Tommy whispers beside me, and I nod briskly in reply. I don't usually go in for cussing, and for the life of me I have no idea what "smoid" means, but if ever there was a time for dropping a few S-bombs, now would be it.

The fluffy white dog closed the door sharply, and once again a loud click rang through the room.

"Zo, you must be little Moose and his fee-line friend Tommy, no?" she asks, clearly not expecting an answer, so I didn't give her one. Tommy, though, wasn't nearly so quiet.

"You must be Tatiana. Q'ute told us you have something important to share with us. Some information about SPECTER."

"Yas," she says, drawing out the word. "But I think she may have misunderstood me a little. Maybe it was my accent, no? What I said was, I have someone I want to share *you* with…"

With that, Tatiana steps over to her left and opens a well-concealed panel mounted next to the door behind her. In the dead center of the panel is a large red lever. Without any hesitation she grabs the level and pulls down hard on it. There's a deep growl of gears grinding on gears, and a large hole slowly begins to open up in the middle of the floor in front of us, stretching from the left wall all the way to the right.

"Welcome to ze new Great White shark display at ze aquarium, Mr. Moose, Mr. Tuxedo. They have come all this way from Australia just to make your acquaintance today. Oh, but I'm afraid someone very naughty has been altering their feeding schedule over ze past few days, so I assure you, ze poor little sharks are ravenously hungry right about now. But don't worry, I'm told they'll take fresh meat any day over another boring bucket of cold dead fish. And you're just ze dog and cat to take ze edge off their little appetites."

Turning back to the panel, she reaches over to press down on a large red button set just below the lever, and the wall behind us immediately starts moaning, the deep moaning sound of almost certain death. I check over my shoulder to see where the sound is coming from, and I can't miss it. The wall is moving toward us, inch by deadly inch!

Tatiana smiles at us, and I swear I can see blood dripping from her fangs. "By ze way, Double O, while you're down there swimming with ze sharks, you might want to take a second to see if there are still any remains left of all ze other agents who've made friends with our lovely little kettle of fish. But make it quick— a second will be just about all the time you'll have to look around before you are consumed by ze majesty of swimming around with all those *beautiful* sharks. Or, I suppose I should say, consumed *by* ze sharks…"

Her shrill laughter shrieked off the walls surrounding us, even as she stretched out her left leg and a claw almost a foot long and two inches wide at the base popped out of her left rear paw.

Shedd Aquarium, Shark Tank

I 've got to give it to Tommy, he thinks on his paws faster than any cat I've ever known. That's probably how he's managed to become so successful over the years, beating all of his competitors to the punch on all those business deals, working his way out of countless tight spots in the process. But I got no idea how he's gonna think his way out of this particular tight spot we've got ourselves in. Or, I should say, think *our* way out of this.

Tommy takes one long hard look at the wall, which is slowly closing the distance between the back of the room and the gaping hole right in front of us where the sharks are no doubt already washing up for dinner. Or whatever they do when it's din-din time. We now have only about three or four feet left before we're both shark bait, so I'm desperately hoping Tommy's got one last good idea left in him right about now.

"Moose!" Tommy's shout gets my attention right away. "Make a step with your front paws, like this!"

He shows me how to link my paws together, kind of like Killer used to do in the old days to help boost me over a tall fence. But I don't get it—the wall that's moving toward us goes all the way to the ceiling, and there's no way he's limber enough to jump all the way across the shark tank—

Tommy grabs me roughly and positions me pointing toward the left wall. I'm just about to ask him what's going on when suddenly he races to the very edge of the tank, then turns and heads my way at full tilt. Leaping and landing with both hind paws on my make-shift booster seat, he scrunches down tight and then blasts out of my arms toward the back wall, a wall that's now almost upon us. Just before he hits the wall, he spins impossibly in mid-air and slams into the wall at full speed, almost near the very top, then springs back way out over the shark tank, landing hard on the other side just inches from the edge.

But Tommy isn't done yet. I'm being shoved ever closer to the tank by the moving wall, my short life starting to flash before my eyes, even as Tommy rolls quickly to his feet and leaps for the control panel on the wall, hitting the red button in full stride.

Immediately I hear the wall that's pressing painfully on my backside grind to a halt, my feet now planted just six inches from eternity. I look up at

Tommy, thinking he's gonna grab the red lever and close the tank, but he's got a whole bunch of other issues to deal with at the moment. The Russian dog clearly isn't happy about what just happened, and has turned on him with that deadly-looking claw of hers.

"*Da. Ty umnyy, a?*" she growls at Tommy in what I guess is Russian, a sound that oozes out of her mouth smoothly, like a purr. She snarls. "A smart one, indeed. So now we get to have a little play date together, no? Why should ze sharks have all the fun?"

With no warning she kicks her left leg sharply in Tommy's direction, and even though he manages to jump back just in time, her claw catches him right across the chest, leaving a bright red line of blood dripping slowly to the floor. I swear I can hear the sharks below us already starting to thrash around, the bright copper smell of Tommy's fresh blood reaching them even down in the water.

Tommy smiles back at her, his canines (or do cats call them felines?) shining dangerously in the harsh light of the room. "My dear Tatiana, I'm afraid I was unaware you were so—*into*—cats. But I'm flattered that you care. Shall we dance, then?"

Tatiana growls and leaps at him once again, and once again Tommy steps nimbly aside just in the knick of time. Again and again she attacks, but after that first cut, none of her slashes with the deadly left claw of hers find pay dirt. Tommy seems to be moving in a wide circle, avoiding her parries, and suddenly I realize what he has been plotting all along. Just a few more steps and he will be back in front of the control panel. And the red lever to the shark tank.

Tatiana apparently saw it, too, and with a quick glance my way, she makes a deft double move and dashes for the panel herself, one paw outstretched for that tiny red button that could put a quick end to my tiny little life.

"Nooo!" I yell, alerting Tommy to the maneuver, but I'm too late. The crazy Russian had gotten the jump on him, and there was no way he could get to her in time before she reactivated the button—and the moving wall pressed right into my back!

I tense for the inevitable, and can't help but hear the sound of sharks leaping out of the water in anticipation of their upcoming meal—ironically, Australian sharks planning to feast on the small but I hoped quite bitter appetizer of a fellow Australian—

when suddenly Tatiana's right foot slips on a slick puddle of Tommy's blood. She tries to correct her fall with her left foot, but the giant claw throws her off, stabbing into the floor and refusing to bend an inch, and instead she slams into the base of the rear exit door headfirst, sending a loud *thwack* bouncing off the walls.

To his credit, Tommy wastes no time taking full advantage of the situation. Grabbing her right rear leg and keeping a sharp eye on the deadly left claw, he swings her around his head in a wide arc, letting go at the very last moment to send her tumbling through the air. And into the shark tank.

Her piercing screams last only a few seconds as the hungry sharks make quick work of the tasty Russian morsel Tommy had just fed them. I can't help but shudder a bit at the sound of them thrashing around down there, enjoying their late lunch, before Tommy turns to the control panel and pushes the red lever back to its original position, and the doors to the shark tank grind mercifully to a close.

Outside Shedd Aquarium

My legs are still feeling a little shaky as Tommy and I make our way out of the aquarium, heading back to Tony's place.

"Too bad she—tanked—before we could get anything out of her about where the Russians are holing up," I complain lightly to Tommy, who smiles lightly at my feeble joke.

"Ah, but that's where you're wrong, my canine friend." He holds up some kind of bulky black box, the back of which is etched with the image of what looks to me like a fat red carrot. "We got this. Tatiana's Beet ePhone. I managed to grab it from her just before I tossed her to the sharks."

Beet phone? Never heard of it. Tommy must have read the confusion on my face, because he leans in closer to me to explain. "It's a Russian knockoff of an Apple iPhone. Ironically made in China, just like most of Apple's products. But a whole lot cheaper. And, as they say, you get what you pay for."

He fiddles with the phone while we walk, almost stepping into an open manhole in the process.

"Hmm, there seems to be some kind of facial recognition security on this thing. Would have been nice to know before the sharks left her face completely—unrecognizable. But maybe Q'ute can make something out of all of this. Unlike her claw, this phone's not exactly *cutting* edge. But it just might wind up being the breakthrough in the case we thought Tatiana was going to hand us, after all."

"So, a side trip back to the labs?" I suggest. All this back and forth is starting to wear me down a bit, but I can see Tommy's point about the Beet phone. If Q'ute can figure out a way to hack into it, it might just cough up one of the few clues we've been able to uncover over the past two days. Or it might cough up nothing more useful than a nasty wet hairball. Hard to really tell with these things.

Q'ute Branch, 2:15 p.m.

Q'ute leads us back into the Sniff room, keeping a close eye out all the while to make sure we aren't being spotted

"A Beet ePhone, eh? Can't say I've ever tried to crack one of those, but I found an XDA forum on the Internet that explains exactly how to do it—those guys can pretty much hack into anything. Let's take a look…"

Glancing back and forth between the phone and a printout of instructions she'd gotten off the web, Q'ute had the phone unlocked in less than a minute.

"So, what do we have here?" she asks herself, clicking quickly through a list of contacts stored on the phone. Finally, near the end, she apparently finds exactly what she was looking for. "Vladimir Kitin. We now have both his cell number and his private pee-mail address. This should be fun!"

Fat Tony's Office, 3:00 p.m.

Tony, Tommy and I are back huddling around the conference room in Tony's office. Everyone else has been cleared out for security's sake.

Tony doesn't look like he's completely buying into the plan yet. "Okay, I guess it makes sense to hit Kitin with the double whammo, where he gets the same message from both Tatiana's phone and from the spy at Q'ute Branch, but why don't we just send him a text message from the phone? Why run the risk of his catching on that it's not Tatiana?"

"We've been over all that, Tony," Tommy answers, a growing irritation starting to show in his voice. "If Kitin has even the slightest suspicion that Tatiana's been compromised, the confirmation message from the mole won't make a bit of difference. He'll just look for an independent source to confirm the whole thing, like calling Boss Dawg directly. And if he does, our plan is doomed from the very start."

"Plus, Q'ute has a program she loaded onto the phone that automatically translates everything that's said from English to Russian. And back," I explain once again. "Just in case Kitin decides to go native on us. And it also changes Tommy's voice to make it sound virtually identical to Tatiana's."

"Plus we'll make the call in front of a really large fan, so Kitin will think it's just the wind garbling everything that's said," Tommy adds. "That will give us cover in case Kitin asks something that I won't have an immediate comeback for. I'll just say I couldn't hear his question because of all the background noise."

Tony has been gnawing at his bottom lip so much I'm beginning to worry about it starting to bleed out. With blood now fresh on my mind, I check on Tommy by reflex, and see that his chest has finally started to scab over, even though we still haven't had a single free moment to get him over to see a doctor. But I'm not sure he cares about that, to be honest. As long as it doesn't get infected, he might just like having a big scar across his chest to show all the ladies.

Tony finally seems to have come to a conclusion. "Okay, I don't like it, but I guess I'll have to go along with the field agents on this one. What's our next step?"

Tommy steps over to a whiteboard hanging on the wall and picks up a marker. The whiteboard is almost immaculate, and I can't help but grin a little when I think about what Tony did to the old whiteboard last year when we were plotting our assault on Southside Prison. I wonder what his master thought when he came in the next day and saw all of the diagrams and mission assignments Tony had laid out on the thing with a nice black permanent marker…

Tommy has started sketching something out, and I need to move over a little so I can see.

"The key to all of this is, we've got to figure out some way to lure both the Russians and the CCs someplace where they'll create a huge problem for the humans, a problem big enough to attract a full-scale response from Chicago Animal Control. If we can get them both together in one place at one time, then bring the humans down on top of their heads, there's a good chance we can kill two birds with one whack. Something I'm pretty good at, actually," he says with a slight smirk.

I have an idea. "So this place, you mean like a dog park or something? That's the only place I've ever seen large groups of dogs wandering around free."

Tommy shakes his head. "No, Moose. It needs to be somewhere that only allows service animals, and no other pets. The airport would be perfect, except I can't see getting two large packs of dogs—especially *big* dogs—through any of the security checkpoints."

"How about a mall or something?" Tony suggests. Easy for the dogs to get inside, and there's a lot of free space—"

"I think you're on to something," Tommy says. "But instead of free space, we need something fairly confining, something that will cause complete chaos. A place where a big dog can't even turn around without crashing into something. Someplace like—" Tommy suddenly goes quiet. He's staring over Tony's shoulder out the picture window, and as I turn to see what he's focusing on, I see it too. A giant sign just a few blocks away. Macy's.

Mullin's Grocery, 4:45 p.m.

Tony and Tommy are busy back at HQ working out the last gritty details of the plan, while I drew the assignment of lining up our team of decoys. And that meant hunting down my old allies, Ike from down on the South Side of Chicago, and Fisheye Martinez, alleyway entrepreneur. Whatever that means.

When we ran into Ike outside the Dead Fish Bar yesterday morning, he said he'd gone into business with Fisheye, and they'd set up shop in the alley behind Mullin's Grocery way out here in Oak Park, in the western suburbs of Chicago. I got lucky hitting all of the right trains, so it took me less than two hours to make the trip out, pulling the old trick Tony taught me about walking onto the train like I belonged there, and sitting halfway between two sets of humans so each of them would think I belonged to the other. It's just not all that hard to fool a human if you give it half a try.

As I make the last turn into the alley behind the grocery, I'm not really sure what to expect. The first time I was here, Fisheye was running a hand-to-mouth operation digging moldy food out of the grocery's dumpster to sell on the street to cats desperate enough to eat just about anything. So when I turn the corner and feast my eyes on what he and Ike have made of the old salvage business, I have to blink twice to make sure I'm seeing things right.

The entire alleyway is a bustle of activity, the whole place swarming with cats running this way and that, tending to their various roles and responsibilities in Ike and Fisheye's new catering business. And not stray cats, mind you, but plump, well-groomed felines—although knowing Ike and Fisheye, I'll bet most of the team were originally recruited right off the streets. Giving a job to those who needed it the most. It's just the way those two cats roll.

I don't really know where to start, but I see a sales counter of sorts off to my left near the old dumpster, so I make my way there.

"Hey," I tell the Calico behind the counter. "Are Ike or Fisheye around here somewhere?"

The Calico gives me a quick, appraising look. "You're a dog."

Obviously, I'm dealing with a real rocket scientist, here. "Yeah, like you said, I'm a dog. Woof woof. And Ike and the Fish are old buddies of mine.

Thing is, I have something pressing I need to talk to them about. They around?"

Calico pauses a long moment to size me up again, then flicks a paw in the air, and a brownish Tabby suddenly appears out of nowhere.

"Franklin, this here—dog—says he needs to talk with the boss." He pauses again, glancing back at me. "Uh—name?"

"Moose," I say, keeping it all tight and to the point.

"Huh. Moose! Figures!" he snorts, then flicks his paw again and the Tabby speeds off into the maelstrom of catering cats. It only takes a minute before I see Ike striding our way, parting the crowd like Moses at the Red Sea, his head and shoulders rising well above all the chaos surrounding him. The grin he's wearing could light up the entire alley.

"Moose! Good to see you! Twice in two days, what a treat! What's up, little buddy?"

"Hey, Ike. I—I need to ask you a favor." I guess I should have led with a little small talk, but time is critical right now. We've got to pull off our ambush before Macy's closes up for the night, and even if Ike agrees to help out with our plan, we're still a good two hours away from downtown.

"Any favor for you would be an honor for me, my frien'. How can I help you?"

He motions me over to a quieter corner behind the dumpster, which is now looking all spiffed up and smelling like fresh-baked bread. Business must be going really good for the two of them these days.

"Ike, sorry to have to drop this on you all of a sudden, but—" Quickly I laid out the situation, and the plan to lure the Russians and the CCs to Macy's downtown. Ike nodded quietly to himself the whole time, letting out just an occasional "uh-hmmm" now and then. When I was finished, he leaned back against the wall of the grocery, thinking.

"You know, Moose, ordinarily this might be a challenge. After all, even if I could round up a team, it's at least two or three hours to get everyone all the way downtown, which doesn't give us much wiggle room timewise to pull this off." He stops and hands me one of his trademark smiles. "But tonight you're in luck! De Fish is already downtown, finishing off a high-dollar catering gig, and he has a team of cats with him who'll be perfect for what you'll need."

"How can we get word to him in time, though?" I ask, feeling a little more relieved. This might actually work!

"Not a problem, mon. Not a problem at all. You just leave dis to me. I got it handled."

Macy's Water Tower, 6:45 p.m.

The original plan was to somehow convince both the Russians and the CCs to meet up here right around seven o'clock, two hours before the store closes, and yet late enough in the day for all the rush hour traffic to die down outside. That would make it easier for the two gangs to find their way to the store undetected, which is key to the whole plan.

Once again, I got lucky with the trains, and it looks like I've made it back just in time for all of the fireworks. I see Fisheye talking to Tommy across the street, probably going over the final details of the caper. Just like old times back at Southside, when we blew a hole in the ceiling of an abandoned sewer tunnel to create an escape route for all the wrongly imprisoned inmates. Now, if we pull this off tonight, maybe we can blow another hole, this time in Vladimir Kitin's plans to put Boss Dawg at the very head of PETSEC, a development that would almost certainly destroy the organization forever. And leave the world a very dangerous place for any animal not lucky enough to have been born a dog.

Tommy seems to be wrapping things up with Fisheye, handing him something that the Fish immediately clips to his collar, and then waves me over as Fish heads toward a cluster of cats gathered in the shadows nearby.

"Moose! Great job getting the decoys lined up on such short notice! I knew you could get it done!"

My ears are turning red at Tommy's words, I know, but that doesn't mean I'm not pleased to hear them. "Aw, I didn't do all that much. Ike and the Fish were just happy to help. Saving PETSEC—that's bigger than any of us. That's bigger than all of us combined."

"You're right about that, Moose. But hey, come on, we've got to get the lead out of our paws. My sentries say the Russians are just a few minutes away, and the CCs should arrive right behind them. It's time we got this show on the road."

He steers me in the direction of the department store's front doors, and using the old trick I'd picked up from Tony for riding the trains, I draft my way inside in between two oblivious groups of humans. Tommy slips in right behind me and points out a spot on the fifth floor near the escalators that will give us a perfect sightline for everything that's just about to go down. We shoot up the escalator largely unnoticed, then take up our positions under a rack of long women's dresses, our eyes and noses just barely poking out from underneath.

While we still have a few minutes left to cool our paws, I decide it would be a great time to catch up on what all had happened while I was gone.

"It was all pretty straight-forward, Moose," Tommy explains to me. "Once we had Vladimir Kitin's contact info, I called him, pretending to be his spy, Tatiana, and told him I—she—had stumbled onto some damning proof that Boss Dawg was planning to double-cross him. Then we sent a similar message to the CCs, passing word to them through the wharf rat me met up with yesterday at the Dead Fish Bar. And then finally we doubled up on all that by slipping a Russian listening device into Boss Dawg's office back at his headquarters, just in time to trigger it remotely to let out a loud, unmistakable squeal so he'd find it right away. Just a mustard seed of suspicion, really, but to a paranoid criminal like the Dawg, that proved to be more than enough."

"And they all bought it?" I ask with no small degree of wonderment. "Just like that? The Russians *and* the CCs?"

"No, not at first. But we slipped a similar kind of back-stabbing message to the folks at Q'ute Branch, hoping the Russian mole would jump on the opportunity to relay it right back to Kitin. Which he did, almost immediately, giving Kitin final confirmation that the rumor was in fact true. And in the process letting Q'ute pinpoint the source of the leak inside the lab, and arrest the traitor on the spot."

"So how does that work to get them all to come rendezvous here?" I ask, already duly impressed by Tony and Tommy's clever subterfuge.

"That part was the easiest of all. We simply sent fake messages back and forth between Boss Dawg and Kitin, arranging for them to meet up here at Macy's in person at seven p.m. sharp to sort through the final details of their sordid plans to throw the election. Just one on one, no henchmen allowed. But of course, each of them promptly ignored that part of the agreement, and as we suspected they've both come loaded for bear. So now we have ourselves a classic face-off between the Kremlin and the Criminal, each of them convinced the other is a double-dealing, no-good four-flushing traitor. Which of course they both are, so where's the surprise in all of that?"

Tommy can scarcely hide the joy in his voice as he lays everything out neatly. But some questions still keep nagging away at me.

"So how exactly do the decoys fit into this scheme? And how does that lead to all the dogs getting arrested somehow?" There are still so many pieces to this puzzle I don't understand, and I can't help but struggle with the notion that Tommy can manage to pull off organstrating so many moving pieces all at once without something going awry.

"Just sit back and watch, little Moose. Just sit back and watch."

Macy's, 6:54 p.m.

The clock is slowly clicking down to seven p.m. Tommy's sentries out front have reported in that Vladimir Kitin is approaching the front door of Macy's, followed by a large pack of Wolfhounds, while Boss Dawg and his gang of Dobermans are only about a block away.

Across the escalator and one floor up from us, a cop with a ginormous gut hanging out over his belt is walking down the aisle near the ladies' lingerie section, this no doubt being the brightest part of his day. Taking a second look, I see that he's not wearing a gun. And the logo on his cap isn't Chicago PD, it's Macy's. So it's not a real cop after all. It's a mall cop.

Then I take a third look. Something about this particular cop seems awfully familiar, but I just can't seem to place it. Then he turns around, facing away from us, and it comes to me right away. Those enormous buns of his, buns I'd sunk all four of my canines into less than twelve months back during the breakout at Southside Prison. It's Officer McFatty! I'd recognize that fat butt of his anywhere! He must have been busted from the force for letting all of those

199

prisoners escape right under his red bulbous nose! Immediately I remember a phrase I'd once heard from Fat Tony a long, long time ago—"Oh how the mighty have fallen."

And just as quickly as that all sinks in, McFatty turns back toward us, and his eyes fall upon me immediately, quickly swelling to the size of saucers as recognition arrives for him as well.

"You!" he screams at the top of his lungs, pointing a fleshy finger at me as he starts running at full speed in our direction. Well, running as fast as those meaty hamhocks of his can take him.

I can't just wait here for him to nab me, and I can't let McFatty's unfortunate presence here destroy our whole game plan for the evening, so I know I have to think of something pretty quick. "Tommy! Gotta make like a tree and bug out! Hold down the fort 'til I get back!"

I back out from underneath the dress rack just as fast as I possibly can, then take off at top speed toward the rear of the store, hoping to lead him away from the coming attractions. McFatty has hit the down escalator at full tilt himself and is taking the moving steps two at a time, holding onto the side rails to steady himself all the way down. As he turns onto our floor he spots me immediately, racing down the main aisle, heading for what I hope is some kind of safe hideout near the back.

Luckily, McFatty's year or so off the Chicago police force fighting the hardened criminal shoplifter crowd at Macy's hasn't done a thing for his conditioning, and as near as he'd come to nabbing me the last time, this time it wasn't even close. Well before he'd finally made his way halfway to the back of the store, I'd already circled around behind him, sprinting just off to his left between the racks, hoping to get close enough to give him a painful reminder of an Aussie Terrier's very best feature—his teeth! But at the very last moment, just as I'm about to spring into action— literally!—he catches wind of me running along right beside him and spins sharply on his heel.

That's when I catch another break. Turns out McFatty is a little out of practice with his ice skating lessons these days, because instead of turning on a dime and bearing down on me at point-blank range, all that blubber he's carrying around his middle swings out hard to the left while the rest of him is swinging just as hard to the right, and both of his feet fly out from underneath him, sending him sliding across the aisle and crashing into a set of mannequins, which fly up into the air themselves and rain down on top of him like a band of zombies enjoying their last meal.

I would have liked to stop for just a second to take it all in, and my sides are already starting to heave painfully with my pent-up laughter, seeing him lying there trying desperately to push the pile of mannequins off of him and getting a handful of miniskirts and activewear tank tops filling his face instead as a reward for all his efforts, but I know I have to get back to Tommy in case I'm needed to help direct all the action downstairs. Duty calls, so with a short little "arf" for good measure, I shoot back down the aisle toward the back of the store—I'd been paying close attention to Tommy when he kept talking about the importance of misdirection—then circle the escalators to finally slide back under the dress rack next to Tommy.

"Good timing, little guy," he whispers, pointing down below us toward the second floor. "Things are just about to get interesting."

Macy's, 7:00 p.m.

I can just barely make them out, Vladimir Kitin and Boss Dawg standing there a few feet from the top of the escalators next to several displays of women's shoes, glaring at each other like gunfighters at the Okey-Dokey Corral. I don't see their goons, but I can assume they're not too far away, hidden like us behind racks of springtime clothing and endless displays of women's socks. Kitin has picked up a shoe from a table off to his right and is starting to pound it slowly onto the table, making a steady rap-rap-rap noise. I don't see any human store attendants at the moment—according to my mistress Helen, you can never find one when you need them—but if Kitin keeps up this loud clatter, I can't imagine they'll stay hidden for very long.

Even with my canine ears I can't quite make out what they're saying, but their body language suggests they had started off arguing with each other rather heatedly, but were now beginning to finally put two and two together and figure out that somehow they'd been had. Within just a couple of minutes, Kitin dropped the shoe back on the table, Boss Dawg pocketed a small cudgel that had appeared in his paw from out of nowhere, and then Kitin reached over and enveloped Boss Dawg in a huge bear hug.

This was all turning out to be a disaster! I glance over at Tommy, who is watching the two men like a hawk, nodding slowly to himself like he had somehow always expected this to happen.

Without warning, Tommy reaches up and taps the side of his collarphone. "T-Man to Fish Leader. It's a go. Release the hounds!"

That's when all hell broke loose.

Macy's, 7:03 p.m.

T hey came out of nowhere, and they kept on coming. Cats! Everywhere you turned, cats! Big cats, short cats, yellow cats, Tuxedo cats, cats with long tails, cats with bobbed tails, giant Maine Coon cats that made Fat Tony look like a midget! Hordes of them! More cats than you ever knew existed!

And just as soon as they appeared, the bottom four floors of Macy's turned into a war zone. If there's one animal Dobermans and Wolfhounds hate more than a stool pigeon, it's a cat, and now Kitin and Boss Dawg's backup armies were completely surrounded by them! This must be what Tommy meant when he said he needed several hundred decoys. He was literally flooding the place with felines, and with fluffy targets surrounding them every which way they turned, the Dobes and Wolfies were completely paralyzed for long a moment, not knowing which cat to chase!

But that only took a moment. Then, just as quickly as they had appeared, the cats suddenly vanished, as only cats are capable of doing. Kitin and Boss Dawg had dropped the man hug as soon as the cats appeared, and were now jerking their heads in every direction at once, wondering what in the heck had just happened. All around them, their minions have crawled out of their hiding places and are scanning the store themselves, hoping to catch sight of just one of those crazy felines, just one unlucky cat they can sink their teeth into.

Meanwhile, the missing humans are no longer missing. Earlier on, when the cats first appeared, a large group of them went screaming down the escalator toward the front doors, while one human had enough sense to pull the fire alarm, setting off a painful wailing sound that almost had me howling back in return.

Kitin and Dawg caught one another's eye, and shared a single word between them—ESCAPE!

But it was far too late for that, because apparently Fisheye's army wasn't quite done with the two thoroughly confused gangs of criminal canines. One by one a random cat would pop up out of thin air to race right under the noses and legs of the dogs, only to mysteriously disappear once again into a rack of clothing just seconds before a vicious canine maw could chomp down hard on its backside. Again and again they leaped out of hiding to taunt the dogs, leaving the canines—and the few humans who were still standing around, their jaws gaping every bit as open as the dogs, but for a different reason—spinning in place, trying to figure out what in the world was going on in the previously tranquil, orderly aisles of the Water Tower Macy's, now less than two hours before closing time. An occasional dog would decide to chase after a cat, despite their apparent lack of success with that strategy, only to crash into whatever display case or rack of dresses and blouses the cat faded into. Pretty quickly the bottom four floors of Macy's looked like a bomb had exploded, the aisles completely blockaded by piles of random clothing and mannequin body parts. On the second floor, a single mannequin head somehow managed to escape its assigned torso only to roll down the main aisle and onto the escalator, where it was carried to the floor below and deposited gently at the bottom, staring sightlessly toward the front door, apparently oblivious to all of the chaos taking place all around it.

Then it happened. One cat on the floor right below us sprung free from its hiding place, but just as it was about to leap to freedom, a truly enormous specimen of Russian Wolfhound rose up in front of its hidey-hole, its mouth already opened wide and dripping with saliva in anticipation of the coming snack. With the way forward no longer an option, the cat miraculously spun to its left in mid-air, landing somehow on the down escalator, just five steps up from the bottom.

The Wolfies were on him in a heartbeat, and for several long seconds the cat and his now completely insane canine attackers ran in place with each other on the rapidly descending steps, canine jowls almost to feline tail, with no one animal seeming to make any headway.

But slowly the dogs began to gain on the cat, and I had to turn my head away rather than watch what was coming to that brave feline, a bloody ending nobody deserved.

And then out of nowhere I hear a familiar voice ring out, and I turn my eyes toward the source of the sound just in time to see Ike standing at the top of the escalator, holding a large roll of red-and-gold ribbon in his paws! Without delay he tosses the roll down the escalator, the ribbon unreeling easily as it bounced quickly down the descending steps toward the bottom. The frightened kitty, sensing his last possible chance to escape his impending doom, immediately sank his claws into the fabric of the ribbon just as soon as it reached him, while Ike grabbed the other end of the ribbon in his teeth and dashed for the back of the store, hauling his friend up the escalator stairs as if the cat had suddenly sprouted wings!

The dogs, seeing their prey snatched miraculously from their mouths at the very last moment, stopped dead in their tracks with shock. Which was a big mistake, because the moving stairway was still moving. Like a growling and revengeful animal, the escalator scooped them up and tossed them furiously to the bottom of the stairs in a giant furry heap. One of the less fortunate Wolfies somehow managed to get the hair of his tail stuck in the mechanism at the bottom, and not knowing how to shut the escalator down, and in a valiant attempt to save him, his buddies grabbed the dog roughly by his collar and pulled, tearing all the fur off the top side of his tail in the process as he howled to the ceiling above in heartrending pain. And, no doubt, heartrending shame.

That episode seemed to have left everyone— humans and animals alike—standing around the store with their mouths hanging slack, breathless and in total shock. And it was at that very moment the cops finally arrived, sealing off all of the exits to the building and pouring in like an invading army hitting a beachhead.

All the cats have now somehow evaporated into thin air, including Vladimir Kitin, but the dogs are all too stunned to put up much of a fight. Soon the cops had them all chained together by their collars and led them docilly outside into a long line of animal control paddy wagons, like the one that took my buddy Killer away, a million years ago. Boss Dawg was the last to go down and was putting up a valiant fight, swinging his claws and snapping his jaws at any copper who dared to come close. But then special agents from the animal control SWAT team arrived on the scene, and it wasn't long before they swatted him with over a dozen nets, keeping him pinned down long enough to hit him with a tranquilizer dart and snap an extra-heavy-duty chain around his gargantuan neck. The Boss didn't look quite so bossy anymore.

Macy's, 7:43 p.m.

With the Dobermans and Wolfies now all under arrest, the mall had finally started to get back to normal. But the cops were still racing around, taking pictures and checking everywhere for any remaining strays, so for the moment Tommy and I were stuck in our hiding place under the rack of women's dresses, waiting it out.

One copper in particular seems to be in charge of the whole operation. He's busy scribbling carefully into a notebook when another, younger cop grabs his attention.

"Hey, Muller, check this puppy out! He's a biggie!"

The cop named Muller strolls over to where three officers are holding down Boss Dawg, who's trapped securely in their three oversized nets, a thick chain clipped onto his black leather collar. Muller's eyes widen like saucers when he takes in the size of the dog.

"Whoa! I don't think I've ever seen a mutt quite that big! You sure he's all Doberman? And not a cross with something else? Like an elephant?"

"Good one, boss!" the first cop chuckles. "But I think he's one hundred percent dog, despite his size. And by the looks of things, the way all the other dogs seem to defer to him, he's clearly the alpha male, here. Head of the entire pack, most likely. Or at least the Dobermans."

Muller slaps a hand on the other cop's shoulder. "Well, good job getting this fella in the nets. He's a handful, for sure. And by the way, whatever you do, don't let him escape. I can't imagine having a brute like that running free down the Miracle Mile. We might have to shut down the entire street if that ever happened."

"Don't worry, boss, we got 'im locked down solid. And I called the animal control guys to bring over another knockout dart to conk him out before we ever try to move him. As big as he is, it'll be hard enough for us to get him up into the back of the truck, even dead asleep."

"Good thinking, officer." Muller leans over to check the cop's name, then scribbles it into his notebook. "I'll make sure you get a prominent mention in my report. Keep up the good work!"

"Thanks, sir!" The copper snaps off a quick salute as Muller walks slowly away from us toward the front entrance to the store, muttering something to himself about canine collusion, all the while scratching feverishly into his notebook with a thick yellow pencil.

Macy's, 8:38 p.m.

With the store finally starting to close up for the day, the coppers took the hint from the store's manager—I think her actual word to them was "Leave!"—and gathered up their equipment and headed back to the stationhouse. That gave us our very first opportunity to climb out from under the dress rack and head home ourselves.

All in all, the night had been a huge success. All of the main honchos from the Crimson Canines were now safely under lock and key, as were what I assume were most of the invading Russian Wolfhounds. With any luck, tomorrow's presidential elections were now safe and secure, as well. The only missing piece in all of this was Vladimir Kitin, the Russian leader. He had somehow managed to slip away from the police dragnet unnoticed and unscathed. And I suppose he was now well on his way back to Russia, with his scraggly little half-hairless tail tucked tight between his legs.

Tommy isn't saying much—I think he's a little disappointed that we didn't catch Kitin, as well. We slowly make our way down to the exits, staying close to the shadows to escape notice from all the humans who are now shuffling about tidying up the racks and exhibits that are lying scattered in the aisles throughout the store. I pass by the mannequin head on the first floor and can't help but giggle when I remember it rolling slowly across the floor and onto the escalator. Looking back, other than that one scary moment with the cat trapped on the escalator, it had been a pretty funny evening. Especially seeing Boss Dawg perp-walked out the front doors and into the paddy wagon. Very funny indeed!

Nobody had locked the front doors down yet, so we're easily able to slip through into the street unmolested, and we turn to head back to Tony's office for a final debrief on tonight's successful operation.

That's when we see him. Vladimir Kitin, staring out at us from the shadows across the street, standing in the framed, gilded entry of a local bank.

Tommy didn't see him at first, not until I nudged him and pointed across the street. And the Russian didn't do anything in response, just stood there staring back at us, like he was somehow daring us to come and get him. Or maybe trying to threaten us in some weird, foreign way.

Now that I have a good look at him, I can tell you I'm far from impressed. I'd expected someone much larger, more commanding, someone like Tommy or Fat Tony. But this guy is a puny little thing—and well named, because if anything, he looked like nothing more than a tiny, scared little kitten.

And his fur! Pretty much his entire chest is hairless, and the fur that he did have here and there is all matted and filthy, like he couldn't give a whiff about his appearance. I mean, even humans know enough to throw on a hat when their hair falls out on top. Would it have killed Kitin to put on a shirt, for goodness sake?

We stand there for several minutes, glaring at each other from our respective sidewalks, when without any warning Kitin tosses us a smirking little salute and then just—dematerializes, just like that! One moment he's there, and the next moment he's not. I can feel Tommy jump ever so slightly right beside me, and realize that I've done the same. It's like we had just seen a ghost. But not just any ghost. A ghost that's likely to haunt us for a very long time.

Home, 6:15 a.m.

Once again my food bowl was waiting patiently for me in the kitchen when I finally struggled home late last night. I could really get used to this whole electronic doggie door thing. It makes coming and going whenever I want to extremely convenient.

And my humans don't seem to mind one bit. They were already in bed and asleep when I arrived, and the house was dark, so I decided to hit the old doggie bed myself. From the smell of things, Helen had moved to the front bedroom for the night, something she almost never does (unless Howard is snoring too loudly, which is almost as disturbing as Bella's barking). I tried her door, but it was shut tight, so I headed back to the master bedroom for the evening.

I must have been extra tired from all of the craziness of the past two days, because I guess I slept in a little. When I finally woke up, the sun was starting to stream into the room—or it may have been the streetlight from right outside our window—and I could hear Helen downstairs, crashing around in the kitchen.

I suppose she was making coffee, which she does nearly every morning, but she's never been this noisy before when she does it. Curious.

I'm still trying to pry my eyes open when I notice that my master Howard is lurking around in a far corner of the bedroom, whispering into his phone. With everything I've learned about the spy business over the past two days, I decide to fake being asleep so I can listen in on whatever it is he's apparently trying to keep hidden from Helen.

"Hey, Phil, buddy. Glad I caught you. You got a minute to talk?"

Phil is our neighbor from next door. Bella's master. I can hear him saying something on the phone, but I can't really make it out. Like I said before, humans have horrible language skills, and it really helps when I can watch their lips move. But I guess that's not an option, here, so I'll have to make out the best I can, trying to fill in the conversation based upon what Howard is saying.

"Yeah, yeah, thanks. I've been working on this promotion for a long time now. Not that Helen cares. All she ever thinks about is that damned dog of hers. Which, by the way, is what I called you about. I understand you're trying to find a new home to dump that little runt of a dog you've got, before the baby gets here—"

Mumbling from Phil—

"No, no, I didn't mean that—I'm sorry, it came out wrong—what I meant was, as you know, with us moving to London in less than a month, I don't know how we're going to manage the whole thing with our dog. I mean, it's tough enough managing the little beast here, where we have a big house and a nice yard, but in London, we'll be living on a boat on the Thames River, and—"

More mumbling—

"Right. Exactly. No place for a dog, for sure. And to make it worse, he's really become quite the bother lately. You heard him howling the other night. No way you couldn't, right? Can't have that, can't have it at all, not on a small boat with neighbors alongside we barely even know. And what's worse, he appears to be sneaking out of the yard again."

Mumbling—

"Uh-huh, just like last year, when he and your dog got out and had us all worried sick. Well, had Helen worried sick. The way she carries on— But, anyway, I was wondering if you had a lead on a good place to take our dog, some bleeding-heart organization that will place him with a new home, with very few questions asked—"

Extensive mumbling. I think I hear Bella's name once or twice.

"Okay, that makes sense. Can't take whatever kind of dog he is to a Corgi rescue. So I guess I'm left with no other option but to hand him over to the pound—"

Mumbling, and it sounds like Phil is excited about something.

"No, I hear you, Phil. But I just gotta think about what's best for everyone around. Helen—she's in no shape to make these kinds of decisions. Whatever organ she uses to think with, it's certainly not her head, you know what I mean?"

More excited mumbling.

"Hey, it was just a joke, okay? I was just trying to be funny. But I—I guess it didn't come out right. Good thing I've got the day job, right? I'd never make it as a comedian."

Quieter mumbling.

"Okay, forget I ever said anything about any of this. I just thought you might have some advice for me, is all. But it sounds like I have a little more homework to do—"

Firm sounding mumbling.

"You're right. I shouldn't do anything rash unless Helen's on board with it. It needs to be a joint decision, for sure. Otherwise, I'd never hear the end of it, right?"

Excited mumbling again.

"A joke!" Howard stops and pulls the phone away from his ear for a second, staring at it with a deep scowl showing on his face. Or what I think is a scowl—it's always so hard to tell with humans. Finally, he puts the phone back to his ear. "Look, buddy, I understand the ladies have arranged for you two to come to dinner over at our place tonight. Let's—let's forget this conversation ever happened, okay? We'll have a few drinks together tonight and put all of this dog nonsense behind us, right? And, hey—good advice about talking it all over with Helen. I think you're spot on with all that."

Quieter mumbling.

"Right. Right. Okay, see you two tonight, then."

Howard sets the phone down on the dresser, then shuffles over to the window and stares outside for a few minutes. Then he glances down at me. I have one eye just barely cracked, but in the dark I know he can't possibly tell that I'm awake and listening. Finally he seems to have made up his mind about something and walks angrily out of the room, grabbing his phone off the dresser at the very last second as he stalks out the bedroom door.

And I know immediately in my gut that Bella and I need to talk. And soon.

Back Yard, 7:05 a.m.

I paused only long enough to finish off my breakfast before rushing out back to unload everything I'd just heard about my master's evil schemes to Bella. If anyone could come up with a plan to somehow get us out of this predicament, it would be her. And with a head as big as hers, that only makes sense.

Bella wasn't outside yet when I made it to the fence, but a few short arfs was all it took to bring her running.

"What do you mean, it's a crisis?" she asks as she pulls up almost muzzle-to-muzzle with me.

I quickly catch her up on everything I'd heard a little earlier. "So it looks like you and I are both being sold on the open market! And from the sound of my master's voice, I might even wind up in some restaurant down in Chinatown!"

"Oh, don't talk like that," Bella cautions me, her ears already starting to do that funny little dance of theirs that happens every time she's trying to sort through a problem. And if ever there was a problem to sort through, this one is epic!

I sit patiently, like I do when I'm waiting for a treat, my butt only wiggling just a tiny bit. Okay, a lot, actually, but I'm really nervous, here. Well above my head, up in the oak tree, I can see Sammy sitting quietly by himself on one of the lower branches, keeping a sharp eye on us. But thankfully he seems to understand this is not the time for playing the old bark-at-the-fence bit. If that's even a thing between us anymore.

Finally, Bella seems to have come to some kind of conclusion. "Okay, what you heard fits in pretty much with everything that's been happening at my house lately. My mistress Susan has been pressing hard to dump me off to the slavers sooner rather than later, while my master has been arguing that they should just wait until their new human puppy gets here and see how it all works out. But I think she's starting to win that argument. From my experience, she almost always wins any arguments she has with my master. She's pretty dogged that way, if you'll excuse my language. Doesn't budge an inch until she gets her way. So that means you and I have very little time left to figure out a Plan B."

"And remember," I add, in full fidget mode by now. "The four of them are evidently getting together for a din-din party tonight. So there's a good chance that might just be a good excuse for finalizing whatever it is they've got in mind. We could be heading off to the slavers as soon as tomorrow morning!"

Bella looks even more worried, if that's even possible for a Corgi. They've pretty much patented that whole worried look thing. "Hmm. I think you may be right about that, Moose. Which leaves us very little time to come up with an alternative solution." She stares over my shoulder for a long moment in the direction of downtown Chicago. "Okay, you're planning on getting together with Fat Tony later today, right?"

"Yeah. The election returns will start coming in around five, and everyone's nervous about how that's going to turn out. But how—" It takes me a second to catch up with where Bella is headed with all this. "Oh! Right! If anyone can get us priority status with PETSEC's relocation bureau, it would be Tony, the newly elected president."

"And he owes you, Moose. Big time. If it wasn't for you, he would already be packing up his office—"

"Well, not exactly, since he's currently still running PETSEC out of his own office, but I get what you're saying. Plus, a lot of the folks over at relo still appreciate what I helped pull off at Southside last year. Saving all those dogs and cats from being put down. So yeah, I'll take off right away and see what I can work out. And with any luck they can figure out how to get us both placed in a good home together!"

"That would be awesome, Moose!" Bella leans over and gives my muzzle a short lick. "If you leave now, you can make it to the office as they are just getting started for the day. That'll give them a whole day to work something out for us. And—Moose." Her eyes are starting to get that wet look again, and it's catching. "I don't have to tell you, Plan B is all we've got right about now. If our humans really are planning to get rid of us first thing tomorrow morning, we won't have enough time to work up a Plan C—"

I nod my head, trying not to look up into those big brown eyes of hers. I need to stay focused here. "I know, Bella, I know. So I guess everything's riding on me now to make this happen, to get the relo bureau working on finding us a new home today, before our masters take us for that final car ride in the morning."

"You can do it, Moose, I know you can. With everything else you've accomplished over the past year, breaking Killer and the rest of the animals out of Southside, saving PETSEC from the Russians and the Crimson Canines, I know you can do it. I—I have faith in you, Moosie. I know you out of all the dogs in the entire world, you can make this happen. Can save both of us from whatever Susan and Howard are cooking up."

Bella's words have finally managed to break through whatever control I've got over my eyes, and I turn my face away quickly before she can see my waterworks in full flow. I'm already starting to work through all the train connections to downtown in my head, and that helps a little with the downpour that's just about to break out on my face. I stumble toward the small hole in the fence behind the mulberry bush and make my way out into the alley. But before I go, I stop to take one long last look at Bella. "You can count on me, Bella," I call out to her in a shaking voice. And I only hope she can. Because if I fail this one last mission, everything else I've accomplished over the last year will have been for nothing.

Relocation Bureau, 9:03 a.m.

I haven't set foot in the relo bureau since the day we got Killer resettled into that nice little house in the suburbs, a day that now seems like a lifetime ago. And in many ways it was. My life now is nothing like what it was before Killer's girlfriend got murdered. For one thing, I had never had to face my own mortality before, never had to stare Death right in his ugly face, eyeball to eyeball. But I did, and I beat him, beat Death, not just once but over and over and over. And now I have to beat a foe even uglier than Death. It's not just about me anymore. I have to save Bella's life.

The dog sitting at the intake desk is so short he can barely see over the top, even though his chair is cranked up all the way to the top, and he's sitting there kind of shivering. Some kind of Mexican short-haired Chihuahua, I think, but this one is mostly no-haired, and what little hair he does have is scattered around his scrawny little body in random little clumps, like someone was gluing it on for him and got distracted. I understand some humans think the breed is so ugly they actually come off kinda cute. Well, there's no accounting for taste, is all I have to say.

I rap a paw on the desk to get his attention. "Uh, excuse me, but I'd like to talk to someone about filing a relo application…"

Chee-wa-wa glances up from whatever he's working on and gives me a sharp and sour look. "You would, eh? Well, mission accomplished, then. You've talked to someone. Now run along, will you. I'm busy, here." With that he drops his attention back to his paperwork.

I clear my throat. "A-hem! What I meant was, I need to get started with filing for relocation. For myself, and for a—friend."

Wa-wa waves a paw toward a rack of paperwork just off to his left without ever once looking up. "You'll find what you'll need over there. Form R-57 to get started. We'll need that in triplicate. When you're done you can just drop it in that box near the door. Someone will get back to you on your application in a few weeks or so if we approve it. Oh, and your friend will need to come down here and apply in person. We don't accept applications from third parties."

Weeks? I don't have weeks, Bella and I will be at the slavers well before that! "You don't understand. I need to arrange a relocation today. And Bella, she can't make it down here to apply. Her humans put a concrete footing around her fence. So no digging out." That wasn't exactly true. They'd missed one particular spot that Bella and I had long ago used to full advantage. But I wasn't going to tell him that.

If anything, Wa-wa seems to have doubled down on whatever he's scribbling on. "Oh, sorry, my bad! I was unaware we had royalty in the building. Read the sign."

He points to a small sign hanging on the wall behind him, then goes back to his scribbling. The sign has a big red oval near the top, with the word "Notice" written inside in bold white letters. Below that in smaller black letters was the phrase "Be Advised: Lack of planning on your part does not constitute an emergency on my part."

Nothing I tried could get Wa-wa to pay the slightest bit of attention to me, and I finally had to give up. Well, not give up entirely. Just go over his head, bring in the big guns. Because this relocation bureaucrat obviously wasn't going to budge an inch.

Fine. I just can't wait to see it when Fat Tony wipes that smug, self-satisfied look off that ugly Chihuahuan face—

Fat Tony's Office, 9:55 a.m.

With the presidential election now winding down to its final phase, Tony is hard at work coordinating something he calls the gotvee effort, whatever that means. Phones are ringing all over the office, and dogs and cats are rushing around like their tails are on fire, so it isn't easy getting him to stop for a moment and listen to my problem. And even then his eyes keep darting around the room and his big hairy tail keeps swishing back and forth, so I know in my heart he's only giving me a very small part of his attention. But that has to be enough.

"So the deal is, I told him it was like a priority, that Bella and I needed something done right away, and he just pointed me to a sign that said he didn't care. Little did he know his boss and I are best buds—"

Tony is only half-listening to my story, nodding slightly the whole time, even as his ears are going every which-way around the room. "Yeah, Moose, I hear ya. Emergency relo… as I've often said, humans are just no damn good, I tell ya. And yeah, I'd really like to help you and Bella out here, I really would, but my paws are kinda tied—"

"But all I need is for you to make a quick phone call, touch base with someone inside the bureau who has the authority to cut through all the red tape, to put Bella and I at the front of the line for relocation."

"Sure, sure. I mights could do that." Someone shoves a piece of paper in front of Tony, which he signs without reading. "Look, Moose, things are kind of crazy here today. Maybe we could pick this up sometime next week—"

"I don't *have* until next week, Tony," I all but shout at him. "Like I said, our humans are probably going to drive us to the slavers tomorrow morning! So we've got to get relocated today!"

"Uh, yeah, I hear your concerns." Another piece of paper snags Tony's attention for a second as he scratches out a signature. "Alright, I'll ask around, okay? See what I can do. But things are a little insane around here right now, so—"

I'm not proud about what happened next, but I was desperate. President or not, it was a matter of life and death. My death, quite possibly. And more important, Bella's. So I grab Tony by his collar and pull him up muzzle-to-muzzle with me.

"You listen to me, *Anthony Shapiro*," I growl as menacingly and convincingly as I can manage, all the while showing every tooth I got. "All of this going on around you right now, this place would be a graveyard if I hadn't stepped up to the plate to save your fluffy little butt. Put my life on the line time after time over this past year to save this organization, to save you. So it's payback time, you hear me? No more excuses—you're going to pick up that phone on your desk and call someone in the bureau, someone who has the power to find Bella and me a new home—*today*—and if you have to, you're going to keeping making phone calls until that happens. *Capisce*?"

I can see his eyes go from angry, to frightened, then all the way to defeated, and I know I've got him.

"Yeah, okay, no need to get ugly here, Moose," he says, finally breaking free from my grip. Off to the side I see some of his security goons moving toward us, but he waves them off. "I'm sorry, I—I'm just a little overwhelmed here, is all. Go on, head back over to the relo bureau. I'll make some calls, and make sure someone sees you right away."

I've cooled off a bit since my explosion, but I'm feeling pretty proud of myself that for the first time in my life I've managed to channel my inner big dog into getting people to show their proper respect for me. Maybe I should try the up front and personal approach a little more often. Like I said earlier, these canines of mine are pretty impressive.

As I pull away I give Tony a little thank you rap on the shoulder with my right paw, then, glaring at his security goons the whole time, just daring them to get in my face themselves, I push my way through the bustling crowd and make my way toward the exit. I can already see that smug little Chihuahua's withering face even as I step out into the sunshine and turn left toward the bureau.

Relocation Bureau, 10:39 a.m.

Once again, Wa-wa didn't even bother to look up from his paperwork, instead just pointing toward a side door and pressing a button under his desk that unlocked the door with a loud buzz.

A large German Shepherd is waiting patiently for me on the other side, and with crisp German efficiency steers me through a rat's maze of cubicles to a large office set in the far wall. *"Herr Moose,"* he announces with a guttural voice as he ushers me though the door, then turns sharply on his heel and strides off briskly down the corridor.

Inside the office, a small dog of highly questionable parentage is rising from his well-upholstered seat behind a large, mostly barren mahogany desk. "Ah, Mister Moose, please come in, have a seat. Can I get you something? A bowl of water, maybe? Milky bone?" He points to another, less well upholstered chair across the desk from him.

I grab the offered chair, hopping up quickly to face him. "No, I'm fine, but thank you." Obviously, whatever Tony had said to whomever it was within the bureau had made a big impression. This champagne and caviar attention is worlds different from the way I'd been treated by that ugly, self-important Chihuahua earlier in the morning. Although, to be honest, I've never tasted either champagne or caviar, so it might be the same after all.

The mutt is speaking, in a high and uncomfortably squeaky voice. "Our mutual friend President Tony has already explained your unfortunate situation to me in great detail. Most unfortunate, indeed, facing the possibility of becoming an unwitting victim of canine trafficking. And your friend, as well. I truly wish we could do something for you, but I'm afraid our paws are tied, here."

That statement hits me from completely out of the blue, like the time my master threw a ball for me to fetch and it slipped out of his hand and careened off the back of my head. "What—what do you mean, your paws are tied? You're the Relocation Bureau! You're ninety percent of why PETSEC even exists!"

"Yes, yes, that's true." Muttsy's ears are now drooping a little from when I'd first walked in. "But, the thing is, relocation is a very delicate and complicated operation. Very scientific, in fact, matching dogs and cats to their potential human masters and mistresses. You've got to place the right animal with the right home and the right humans at the very precise moment the prospects for adoption are at their highest. If any of those things is just the slightest bit off, it just won't work. And the trickiest part of all of that is the human target, catching them at the very moment they feel weak enough to want to take in a stray off the street. You saw how it all works, when we placed your friend Killer in that home with the little girl. It all has to be very carefully choreographed to make sure everything clicks into place at just the right point in time. No room at all for error."

"But with all the resources you have at your disposal, surely you can find something, someone who's willing to take Bella and me in," I protest. "We're very good dogs, and very desirable breeds at that."

Muttsy nods his head slowly, but I can tell he's not convinced. "You are that, for sure. Normally, any human in their right mind would jump at the chance to adopt a well-behaved Corgi and a Yorkie, but—"

On any other day I would have torn his half-breed face right off his skull for that insult—Yorkie, indeed!—but today I have to hold my bark. I need this guy on my side, at least until Bella and I can get situated in our new home. "But what?" I ask, not completely succeeding at keeping all of my one-inch canines hidden from view. "Can't you at least locate two families who live right next door to each other, like we have now? Is that so hard?"

"Actually, Mister Moose, it is, it really is. You see, before you arrived for this meeting I had my computer boys run a scan of our databases, where we store all of the info on potential human targets, and not only do we have zero possibilities on the two-dog adoption angle, it seems we don't even have two high-profile humans that might fit the bill living anywhere near each other. Much less two human families who are a good match for your two breeds."

"Then just place us with anyone who's close! That'll save us from the slavers for now, and you can re-relocate us later on when you find a perfect match!"

"I'm afraid it doesn't work that way, Moose. I'm sorry, but our entire operation is predicated on our target humans being already highly susceptible to the adoption. And the adoptees. We tap into their television feed and insert specially designed ads featuring cameos of the very type of dog we're trying to place. We arrange for them to 'randomly' run into other humans with the same breed of dog over the course of several months, while we try and steer other breeds away from them. And that's just a small sampling of the psychological tricks we have in our arsenal. Our experts on human behavioral training call all that the Baader-Meinhof phenomenon, or more commonly, confirmation bias, flooding their tiny human brains with images of other humans enjoying something they don't yet know they want. In this case, a dog or a cat. And it works almost every time, kind of like when dogs see other dogs with a bone. There's no thought process involved, they just gotta have it."

"Then just batter my hoof for Bella and me! Why can't you do that?"

"Because—the Baader-Meinhof approach doesn't work overnight, it takes time. Sometimes many weeks or even months before we've rendered the humans sufficiently susceptible to the adoption. A single day? That's barely enough time to get them to jump on something they're already convinced they want, like an expensive car or a good steak dinner. You see, humans have this stupid habit of wanting to 'sleep on' things overnight before they make a decision.

But—if you're right about what your masters are planning, overnight will be one night too many to keep you from being handed off to the slavers. I'm sorry. I wish I had better news."

My stomach is starting to roll over, and suddenly I feel like I might dump this morning's breakfast all over the spotless desk in front of me. Weeks? Months? Bella and I just don't have that kind of time. Even if it doesn't happen tomorrow, I saw the look in Howard's eyes. It's all just a matter of time, whether I like it or not. So I need to figure out a Plan C, after all. And fast.

"Okay, so what's our alternative here?" I ask. "Say you get to work on a relo for Bella and me today. What do we do to escape the slavers in the meantime?"

Muttsy's ears droop even further. "I—I'm afraid our only option is for you and your girlfriend to hit the streets before you get shoved into your masters' cars for that final trip to the slave factory."

"You mean run away from home? Become— homeless? Run-of-the-mill strays? Is that what you're saying?" I can't believe what I just heard. I mean, I have a lot of recent experience with the dark and dangerous mean streets of Chicago, so I would make out just fine. But Bella? Whole different story. Bella is a city dog, used to all of the comforts of home. She wouldn't last a day.

Muttsy slaps both paws down hard on the desk in front of him, startling me. "Strays? We—we don't like to use that term. It's all so—derogatory. We prefer to call them 'fenceless.' As in unfettered by human barriers, by human limitations and expectations. Free to roam wherever their hearts might take them. As all the breeds were back in the very beginning of time, before we had masters and mistresses to serve us."

I'm having none of that. "Yeah, like I said. Strays. Stuck out on the streets with no idea where our next meal is going to come from. Sounds like a real peachy keen idea."

"Well, when you put it like that—"

"And you know how that all ends up for us dogs in the end. Scooped up by the animal cops and thrown into prison like Killer. Until the grim reaper swings by on Monday morning and—" I make a sign like a knife cutting my throat.

"No, no, it's not like that in Chicago anymore! The city has adopted a no-kill policy—"

"Right. Bella told me all about that. No-kill. But they really should call it some-kill, shouldn't they? Because they still get to kill as many as one out of five dogs—"

Muttsy's ears are now pulled straight back, because he knows I'm right about what is really going down out there. "Uh, well, maybe in some of the prisons... but you and your girlfriend, there are rescue groups for your breeds, so you wouldn't have to worry—"

"So only the less desirable dogs get offed, like my pit bull friend Killer? Yeah, I get it." This conversation is going nowhere fast. Leaving me with the distinct feeling that I need to be somewhere else even faster. Somewhere where I can find some answers, instead of listening to this overpaid waste of good kibble—

Muttsy stands up abruptly and pushes a card across the desk. "Look, I'm sorry I can't make things happen any faster, but here's my personal number. Stay in touch. As soon as we know something—"

"You'll give me a call. Got it." Not the first time I've heard *that* one. "Okay, well I guess we're done here. I've got to get back to HQ and help out with the election. So you can still have a job tomorrow morning, such as it is." I flick my tail at him and hop off the chair. But before I leave, one last little thing is nagging at me.

"You said PETSEC prefers to call stray dogs 'fenceless.' Do they also have a name for the dogs that do have good homes?"

That seems to throw him for a second. "Uh—I suppose maybe you might call them *de*fenceless…"

Yeah, that makes a whole lot of sense. Stuck inside a nice, safe home, with two solid meals a day, lots of humans to wait on you and dish out endless full body massages… and free healthcare to boot! Being defenceless doesn't sound like all that bad an idea right about now. So I guess I just gotta find Bella and me a good fence to hide behind. And I'm rapidly running out of time to do it.

Miracle Mile, 11:30 a.m.

With absolutely no idea what Bella and I are going to do about our current situation, I figure at least I could drown my sorrows by staying busy helping out with the election. I'm only about a block from Tony's office when I bump into Tommy on the street. Literally. One moment I'm dodging some idiot kid racing down the sidewalk on an electric scooter, and the next I slam right into him and go sprawling.

"Ooof! Watch it you stupid—" When Tommy finally rolls his eyes in my direction and sees me lying there, trying to sort out up from down, he immediately jumps up and starts to apologize. "Hey, sorry, Moose. I—"

"No, you're right, Tommy. I had my eye on that knucklehead with the scooter, and I should have been paying closer attention to where I was going."

"Yeah, same here. The fool almost ran me over, too. He came from out of nowhere with that thing." Tommy stretches out a paw to help me up. "So where are you headed off to in such a hurry this morning?"

I point down the street in the general direction of Tony's office, ground zero for all the election activity today. "Just checking in to see if I can help out in some way. I wanted to sit in on the election returns later on today, so running home and then turning right back around didn't make much sense."

"Well, if you'd like you could hang out with me. I've been sent on a mission to check out a few reports of voting irregularities at some of the polling places. Feel like taking a little stroll?"

"Sounds like a great idea, Double-O. Lead on!"

As we saunter down the street I fill Tommy in on my problems at home, and the possibility that Bella and I might wind up homeless as early as tomorrow morning.

Tommy rests a reassuring paw on my shoulder. "Hey, buddy, don't sweat it. If you and the girl wind up on the street, maybe you can come work for me for a while. I don't think we have any openings right now, but things do pop up from time to time. And I'll warn you, it doesn't pay all that much, but it'll keep a roof over your head and kibble in your bowl until something better comes along. I can certainly use a resourceful dog like you on the team."

That is absolutely the best news I've heard in days! But then I remember the part about "no openings right now." Not so best news after all. "Uh, thanks for the offer, Tommy. That'd be swell. If something bad does happen at home, you'll be the first person I'll call for sure."

"Don't mention it, Moose." Tommy stops suddenly and gives me the evil eye. "And by the way, I mean that. Don't mention it. Ever. Otherwise I'll have every freeloader from here to Wisconsin sniffing around my office looking for handouts like it was free cheeseburger night at the Sonic."

"No. Right. My lips are sealed." I make the zipper motion on my muzzle to let him know I'm serious.

We have just crossed the bridge over the river, my steps a bit lighter now, when all of a sudden I hear a little *whoosh*, and something whizzes past my right ear and imbeds itself deep in the trunk of a tree in front of me. Whatever it is, it's pretty tiny, really, with tiny little feathers to match, almost like some kind of dart.

"It's a poison dart!" Tommy yells, grabbing me by the shoulders and pulling me quickly into the safety of a nearby crowd of humans. "The Russians! They're onto us!"

I check back over my shoulder, and sure enough, several Wolfhounds are hot on our trail and closing fast. One stops and puts a long tube of some sort up to his lips, and a second later a human right beside me screams out and collapses onto the street.

"This way!" Tommy shouts, already racing headlong down a steep set of steps leading toward the river.

I'm right behind him, but as we near the bottom, I'm starting to worry that Tommy may have led us into a trap. A dead end, quite literally in this case. But then he veers left and leaps on board a small boat that is just pulling away from the pier. I redouble my speed and barely make it on board myself.

"We're safe!" I holler at Tommy over the din of the boat's engines. Behind us I can see that the Russians have made it to the pier as well, and I'm just starting to feel good about our chances of making a great escape when without any warning one of the dogs jumps on board another boat and butts its human owner over the opposite side and into the water. Within seconds the other Wolfhounds have joined him on board, and I head the distinctive sound of the boat's engines coming to life. They're after us again!

And that isn't our only concern right now. From the front of the boat I hear a loud shout and another human starts running toward us, waving his arms wildly.

"Moose! Follow me!" Tommy darts toward a small hatch near the rear of the boat, disappearing into it in a flash. I'm right behind him again, leaving the human still shouting at us from up above.

Wherever it is we landed, it is really dark down here, but things start to get a little clearer as my eyes finally adjust to the light. Glancing around, it appears to be some type of room for mechanical equipment, and by the sound of the huge machine chugging away beside me, I can guess that we've located the boat's engine.

Tommy has zeroed in on a spyhole at the very back of the boat and is staring intently through it, trying to make out what's happened to the Russians.

"They're right behind us, Moose. And they're gaining on us! A few more minutes and they'll be right beside us. We've got to figure out some way to make this tug go faster."

He pulls away from the spyhole and examines the engine with an appraising eye. "Aha! Just what I need!" he yells, reaching for a funny-looking lever that's attached to a long metal wire stretching off into the distance toward the front. "It's the throttle. Here, Moose, give me a hand."

Tommy snatches a wrench off the floor and is using it to push hard on the lever thing, motioning for me to help out with it. With a tremendous effort we manage to shove the lever forward all the way to the stops, and the boat's little engine screams beside us in protest as our ride instantly leaps forward, the nose of our boat rising ever so slightly into the air. Tommy jams the wrench in place, then jumps back to the spyhole.

"Perfect! We're opening up a lead on them. Now let's just hope the driver up there can keep us from crashing into something."

I was so excited about making our escape that I hadn't even thought about that possibility. If we hit something dead-on going at this speed, it'll be all over for us, for sure. We might be done in even before the Russians get to us!

I poke my head up through the hatch to check out what's happening up top. Maybe if we could see the wreck approaching, we could jump off the boat just in time to save our necks. In the front of the boat, the driver is trying to pull back on the throttle with one hand while steering the boat with the other, but it doesn't take him long to figure out he needs to keep both hands planted firmly on the wheel.

Beside us, other boats whizz past in a blur like they're stuck in reverse, and several times we shoot between two or three boats so close I can actually see the paint peeling off the sides of their bows. Off on the shore, people are pointing at us and shouting as we race past. My ears are flopping crazily in the wind, but somehow that doesn't feel quite the same as it does when I stick my head out the window of Helen's car.

I look back again, hoping against hope that the Russians have decided to give up the chase, and I'm shocked to see they are now bearing down on us again, and closing the distance between us in no time! They seem to have lucked out by stealing a much faster boat, and it's now only a matter of minutes before they'll be onto us!

I duck back down inside the hatch. "Tommy!" I shout, pointing in the direction of the Wolfhounds' boat.

"Yeah, I know," is his simple answer. "But we're already going every bit as fast as this thing can take us. We've got to think of some way to stop them, and fast!"

As Tommy was talking, we must have hit a wave or something, because the boat flew a foot or so into the air, then crashed down hard on the water, sending me flying against the side of the engine. By sheer instinct I throw out a paw to brace myself, and wind up grabbing something just before impact that gives ever so slightly. Before giving way completely.

Immediately the engine coughs and sputters, then dies entirely. We're now stuck dead in the water with no power, with the Russians racing our way at full throttle! And if we don't think of something pretty quick, in just a few minutes we'll be every bit as dead as this engine!

"What did you do, Moose?" Tommy yells, but almost immediately the answer is crystal clear—my collision with the engine had torn loose a fuel line, and gasoline is now flooding the compartment. I start to gag from the fumes, but Tommy quickly leaps on the hose that is thrashing round the tiny room like an angry snake, spraying gasoline everywhere. He grabs the snake by its head, then spins around and shoves it through the spy hole. The hose is bucking in his hands like a wild animal, and it's everything he can do right now to hold it in place.

"Moose, see if you can find a red box of some kind It should be in here somewhere—"

Instantly I see it! There, on the shelf! I grab the box and toss it to Tommy.

"No, no, not a first aid kit. The flare gun, Moose! Quickly!"

I root around the gasoline-soaked shelves searching for another red box even as I hear the sound of another boat engine, slowing down, right on our rear. Then I see it.

"This what you're looking for?" I ask, sliding the box across the floor toward Tommy. If in fact there is a gun of some sort locked inside that box, no way I'm going to be throwing it through the air!

"Perfect!" Still holding the hose in place with one paw, Tommy flips the latch on the front of the box and pulls out a pistol with a really fat barrel. He grabs something else out of the box and loads it into the gun, then pokes the barrel out through the spyhole and pulls the trigger.

Chicago River, 11:57 a.m.

I don't know what I was expecting from that tiny little gun, but the blast it set off was like Tommy had just fired a massive cannon out the back of the boat. Something like a ginormous hand slammed into the back of the boat, sending us flying, then a fierce red light instantly flooded our little engine room, followed immediately by a furnace-like blast of hot air.

The back of our boat is now leaking dangerously, filling the tiny engine compartment with water. Tommy scrambles up the hatchway, motioning furiously for me to follow. And motions are pretty much the only way to communicate at the moment—the explosion had left my ears ringing like church bells on Sunday. Which for some reason had my mouth watering like it was time for Sunday dinner.

When we get back on top, I glance back at the Russian boat, expecting them to be jumping on board our ship at any moment, armed to the teeth with knives and swords, ready to slash our throats. But strangely, their boat is now nowhere to be seen, just a ton of random debris floating around in the water behind us, and a half-dozen Wolfhounds dog-paddling desperately to stay afloat.

The driver of our boat seems to be trying everything in his power to turn the boat around to help rescue the Russians, but with his engine completely kaput and his boat rapidly taking on water, he finally abandons the idea and instead grabs a rope and tosses it to another boat that has pulled up alongside, hollering to them that he needs to be towed right away to the wharfs that are stationed way off to our right. With the tow line secure and the two boats puttering slowly toward shore, he takes off for the back of the boat and jumps down into the engine room, trying desperately to save his own boat from drowning in the flood of river water that is seeping through cracks caused by the explosion. He tosses us an angry, accusatory look as he races past, but I think he's way too concerned about his boat at the moment to pay us much mind.

Nevertheless, we're not in any position to deal with him ourselves at the moment, so as soon as the boat sidles up next to the wharf we waste no time leaping to freedom and disappearing into the huge crowd that has gathered to watch the boat chase and explosion on the river. I'm sure it's a sight none of them have ever seen before, even in their wildest imaginations. And I can assure you it's something I don't want to experience ever again. As Fat Tony reminded us once, it doesn't matter whether you're a dog or a cat. You only live once.

Fat Tony's Office, 5:30 p.m.

With the Crimson Canines and their loathsome boss now locked up safe and sound in the newly rebuilt Southside Prison, we can finally take a break to check on the election returns. And I'm unpleasantly shocked to see that Tony is running pretty far behind Boss Dawg in the early polls. And even more shocked to see that he doesn't seem bothered by that fact in the slightest.

"Do you know something I don't, Tony?" I ask him when we finally get a moment to talk quietly face-to-face.

"Well, that goes without speaking, Moose," he answers with a grin. "But then, 'something' is a pretty broad topic. Do you have anything specific in mind?"

It takes me a second to catch the insult. Tony is clearly getting back to his cocky old ways. At least as far as I'm concerned. You would think he'd show me some gratitude—and now I'm not all that sure I care whether he is losing or not. Except when I remember the alternative…

"What I meant, Tony, is that the returns have you trailing Dawg by quite a large margin. Do you expect that's gonna change at some point? Maybe the late returns will swing the numbers around for you somehow? Maybe a surge out in the western suburbs?"

Tony laughs, an easy laugh that manages to jiggle most of what's left of his belly fat. "No, no, Moose, thanks to our Russian friends, the numbers will probably just get worse as we get further into the night. Q'ute tells me they hacked all of the polling machines, making sure Boss Dawg got almost all of the votes. But of course, none of that matters at this point."

"Why's that? Don't you want to win the election?" I'm now completely confused by his attitude, which is just the opposite of what I would have expected from him. Especially after everything we had just been through over the previous two days, trying to save the election. Tommy and me, especially.

Tony is still grinning mischievously like that Cheesy Cat from the Alice stories, even as a shout goes up from somewhere out in the crowd and new numbers are updated on the whiteboard behind him. Even further behind! "Of course I want to win it, Moose. That's never been in doubt. I want to win it not just for me, but for all the doors it will open for all the other cats, all over the world. But—why don't we let Tommy explain it to you?"

I hadn't noticed Tommy slipping up behind me, a giant smile plastered on his own flat face.

"Moose! Come grab a drink! It's time to celebrate!"

"But—but Tommy, what is there to celebrate? We're losing to the Dawg by a landslide!"

Tommy shoots a sharp look in Tony's direction. "What, you haven't told him?"

Tony shakes his head. "No, why don't you do the honors?"

My eyes keep flicking back and forth between them like I'm watching a Chinese ping pong match. What in the world is going on that I'm just not getting?

Tommy swishes his long black tail and stretches out a paw to place lazily on my shoulder. "Okay, Moose, it goes like this. Have you ever had a chance to study PETSEC's Constitution? Particularly the section on how presidents get elected?"

I shake my head no. Reading is something I try to avoid at all costs. Like baths.

"Well, then, that's why you're confused by all this. You see, my friend, when our Founding Canines first drafted the Constitution, they were concerned that some scallywag at some point down the road would figure out a way to get elected to the presidency despite his lack of—the proper *character*, shall we say—and then misuse the powers of his office in various nefarious and unforeseen ways. To escape prosecution for all his crimes, maybe, or perhaps provide pardons for all of his cronies. Or even sell the spoils of his office to the highest bidder. Which was pretty prescient of them, because that is almost exactly the problem we were facing with this election. Boss Dawg taking over PETSEC and using it as his own private fiefdom, that is truly a scenario from hell. So, to keep this from ever happening, the founders stuck in a few important safeguards."

"More than a few, actually," Tony adds with enthusiasm. "Unlike the human Constitution, which is chock full of vague and contradictory provisions, ours was always intended to serve as an airtight shield for justice and democracy. Or nearly airtight—as we just almost learned to our detriment."

Tommy continues his explanation, and I have both ears trained on him like laser beams. "Exactly. As you know, Moose, nothing is perfect, no matter how hard you try to make it so. But the framers of our Constitution put in clauses that, like the humans, allowed presidents to be ousted from power if Congress found them guilty of 'high crimes and misdemeanors.' But unlike the humans, we also added in a clause that prevents any animal currently serving time for 'high crimes and misdemeanors' from ever getting elected in the first place. And, if the crimes happen to involve some kind of plot to steal the election, or any other unlawful electoral scheme, that ban is perpetual."

A light is starting to go off inside my head. "So when Boss Dawg got arrested last night and thrown into Southside Prison—"

Tommy's tail is swishing nonstop now. "He was automatically rendered ineligible to participate in the election for PETSEC president."

"And that means I was the only candidate still left on the ballot, so I was the only one who could get elected," Tony cuts in with a wicked grin. "Boss Dawg's votes get thrown out as a matter of law, and I win the election by default. Regardless of how the Russian hackers managed to rig the voting machines."

Now it all suddenly makes sense. "And the whole chaotic mess at Macy's—"

Tommy spreads his paws out wide in front of him. "That was all a carefully executed plot to get Boss Dawg arrested just in time to erase his name from the official ballot."

"And we'll be bringing our own criminal cases against him very soon in PETSEC federal court, charging him with conspiring with the Russians to steal the election," Tony explains. "So, according to our Constitution, he will forever be banned from holding any office of any kind within PETSEC. He can't even be elected human catcher by the time we're finished with him. That is, assuming he ever gets released from Southside, which I sincerely doubt will ever happen. I can't see any human ever thinking he might make a nice lap dog for some kid."

"So what happens to the Crimson Canines, now?" I ask.

Tommy shrugs his shoulders. "My best guess is they'll just melt away, whatever's left of the organization. Without Boss Dawg keeping everyone in line, it's not exactly a group of well-behaved model citizens we're talking about. None of them have ever developed much beyond the puppy stage, emotionally or intellectually. And you know how well-organized puppies can be."

As a former puppy myself, I guess I should have been offended by that remark, but Tommy has a good point. And I can only hope he winds up being right about all that. Boss Dawg or not, the Crimson Canines have caused a world of sorrow and anguish to humans and animals alike over the years, and I for one won't be sorry to see that group of rabid canines disappear from our city's streets for good. Or should I say, for bad?

Home, 6:30 p.m.

Now that I know the election's in the bag, there's no real reason to hang around Tony's office any longer for the celebration, and I desperately need to get back to Bella. She's probably worried sick right about now, thinking she might be trafficked to the slavers as early as tomorrow morning. And I'm not all that sure she's gonna feel any better after what I have to tell her.

Bella's waiting for me by the fence the moment I arrive home, her eyes filled with that combination of sad puppydog, loyal companion look only a Corgi could really pull off. Sammy Squirrel has moved down from the tree and is sitting on top of the fence as I crawl through my hole under the mulberry bush. Which, by the way, is getting a lot harder than it used to be—is it possible my little escape hole is starting to shrink up on me?

Sammy starts chittering away almost as soon as I squeeze through. "I must say, Moose, I'm impressed by what you managed to pull off over the last two days. Didn't really think you had it in you!"

I'm not sure whether I should take that as a compliment or a back-handed insult, but since Sammy's got no hands, I decide to go with the former. Anyway, the Squirrel's the least of my problems at the moment. I gotta face Bella with the bad news.

She hits me with it right off the bat. "So, what did you find out, Moose? Does the Relo Bureau have something lined up for us yet?"

Slowly, and very delicately, I walk her through my day and my fruitless meetings with the good kind folks from the Relocation Bureau. There's just no way to sugarcoat the news—unless some miracle pops up literally overnight, Bella and I are completely out of options. By this time tomorrow we'll probably both be homeless and starving, living each day paw-to-mouth. In other words, strays. I'm just not going with "fenceless."

Bella looks completely devastated. "I—I don't know what to do, Moose! I overheard my humans talking just this afternoon, and Susan was really adamant about sending me off to some prison farm, or maybe some place even worse, and I think my master is starting to cave under all the pressure. What's worse, I think they're coming over to your house tonight for dinner. So if something's afoot between Susan and your master Howard, my guess is they'll spring it on Phil and Helen tonight, probably after they've gotten them loosened up with that silly juice they always drink. We need to be there when it happens, find a way to listen in on what they're planning without any of them knowing we're there!"

Bella and I are on the same page on all this right now. I think back to earlier today, on the boat. If what we're facing is in fact a life-altering collision in our lives, then we need to see that crash coming soon enough to jump free in time, stray or no stray

"Okay, Bella, here's the plan. I'll sneak you inside through the doggie door as soon as Helen's served up what she calls her appeteasers. Everyone will be in the living room at that point, so we can set up a steak out under the dining room table. That's where I always like to hang out when there's steak out—close to the action where I can grab a mouthful or three when nobody's looking."

"I don't think that's what they mean by the phrase 'stake out'," Bella murmurs. "But go on. What happens when they move into the dining room? They'll expect you to be there, to be sure, but if anyone ever thinks to check under the table they'll spot me in a heartbeat."

"Right. So that's when we'll swing back through the kitchen and wait near the butler's pantry for Helen to drop off the first set of plates and then grab the dinner plates and start shuffling them toward the dining room. I'll distract her by doing my little dancing, begging routine—she falls for it every time—while you scoot over beneath the breakfast table. The lights will be off over there in the corner, so you'll be completely in the dark, unseen. When all the humans are finally in the dining room, I'll signal for you to slink across the living room to take up a scouting position under the couch while I keep them distracted by trying to jump in everybody's laps. When you're safe and sound and I've gotten more than my fair share of 'bad dogs', I'll pull the old misdirection switcheroo back through the kitchen and then join you under the couch. How does that sound?"

"Wow. You really have picked up some skills as a Double-O agent over the past few days," Bella gushes. And I'm not going to lie, my chest has swollen right now to about double its normal size. No way I'd make it through that hole near the mulberry bush now.

Okay, back to the steak out. With the plan now in place, all we have left is to execute. My supersensitive ears pick up Bella's humans walking out their front door, heading toward my house, so we don't have a second to waste. It's launch time.

Home, 9:30 p.m.

My plan worked out to perfection, I'm happy to say. That whole organstraw thing I wasn't sure Tommy could pull off? Well, I had the fat lady singing all night long. No one had the slightest idea Bella was even there. Or that the two of us were steaked out spying intently on their conversation the whole time.

Not that it really mattered. As usual, the humans spent the night mangling their words like they all had a fistful of marbles in their mouths, and Bella and I barely understood a word they said. The silly juice didn't help.

Finally, Bella's humans said their goodbyes and stumbled home. And by stumbled, I mean that quite literally. Phil was totally wasted, and he was getting an unwelcome earful from Susan. And, hey, I hate to pull the old superiority thing on humans, but you know, it is totally irresponsible of them to behave like that when they know they have their real responsibilities back home making sure we're completely protected and well served. Just saying.

Anyway, Phil and Susan have just left, and Howard and Helen are back in the living room, while Bella and I have shifted steak out positions and are trying to stay invisible under the dining room table. Which took no small amount of planning on my part to organstrate, I might add.

For the second night in a row, my humans seem to be really upset at each other, this time apparently about something that was said over dinner. Something neither Bella nor I managed to catch, despite our best efforts. We both have our ears up and fully locked in, trying to figure out what the argument is about. And to make things worse, I have a second, equally pressing concern—I need to get Bella back home safely and completely undetected, and soon. We don't need to hand Susan any more ammunition to fire Phil's way. Not now, not when everything's on the line.

Howard is talking, his face beet red, his right fist pounding the space above his head like he's playing some kind of Air Whack-A-Mole. Helen does not look happy at all.

"What the hell, Helen. First Moose, and now this? You have got to be kidding me!"

"I think it's a perfectly good solution, Howard. Everyone benefits. It's a win-win proposition all the way around."

Howard turns on her, now pulling his fists down to his side. "And just how is this a win-win, Helen? I relented and gave in to you on the Moose situation, okay? Thinking that might make you happy, just trying to be understanding, right? But now you just seem to be doubling down on me all of a sudden. Two dogs? Not going to happen. Not in my lifetime."

"First of all, mister, if you relented on the whole Moose thing, this is the first I've heard of it. The last word I heard out of your mouth on the subject is that you were dead set on taking him to the pound. Which is never going to happen, by the way. Never—going—to—happen."

"Don't try and change the subject, Helen. Moose or not, no way we're hauling a second dog across the pond. A dog, by the way, that her own owners don't even want. Want to dump her the first chance they get. Well, this ain't the city dump, Helen. We got our own load of trash to deal with, is all I'm saying."

"Trash? *Trash*? You're saying Moose is nothing more than *trash*?" I seldom see Helen out of sorts, acting anything other than completely poised and in control, but now she seems like she's ready to explode any minute now. Maybe even commit murder. Her hands grab the sides of her thighs, squeezing hard, in a way that has got to be painful. Finally, staring off in our direction but not seeing Bella and I watching her from under the dining room table, she responds in a strangely quiet and tightly controlled voice. "Actually, I don't recall my ever giving you a vote in the matter, Howard. But you want me to be a housewife? Fine. Then it's my decision to make. Housewife, that's two simple words. House, wife. So if that's what you want me to be, if that's the role I'm supposed to play, then fine. I will. But that means it's my house, my household, so it's my rules. I'll run it however I please. Case closed."

"No, Helen, decisions like these are not unilateral. We have to agree—"

"Like I agreed for you to take the new job? Like I agreed to move off to some foreign country and live on a damned boat? I'm sorry, refresh my memory. When exactly did those votes occur?"

"The new job in England is the very best thing that could happen for the both of us, and you know it, Helen. The money—"

"When was the last time you heard me complain about being poor? When was the last time you heard me complain about needing more money? This isn't about the money, and it never has been. It's about you, and you alone. I've never even been consulted. You'll recall that the first time I even heard about the new job was *after* you'd accepted it."

"They needed an answer right away—"

"And you couldn't even put them on hold and give me a call first? Did you even think about me *once* before you said yes?"

"I thought you'd be thrilled about the whole thing, a chance for an adventure—"

"No, don't even try to go there, mister. Look, I've told you what I think about all this. I'm not yet ready to break up our marriage, not at this point. But you need to make some big changes in your behavior toward me, Howard. You need to make some serious changes in your whole attitude toward me. And it all starts here. I've made up my mind, and I'm not going to discuss it any more. Period."

"But, be reasonable, Helen. The noise—how can anyone possibly deal with that kind of cacophony in such a tiny, confined space?"

But Helen has the same look on her face she was showing the day she beat the Doberman out of our back yard with a broomstick. Her arms are crossed, tightly, and she's refusing to even glance in his direction. My master Howard makes his way slowly over to the front of the fireplace, leaning forward with his hands on the mantle, staring smolderingly into the smoldering fire. Finally he stiffens, standing up straight and throwing both hands into the air.

"Okay, okay! I give up, Helen! You win! We'll take the damned Corgi with us to London. The Corgi and that damned Yorkie of yours. And it's on you, Helen, it's all on you. I'll have nothing to do with either one of them!"

I only caught a few words of what had been going back and forth between them, mainly focusing in on the body language, but I clearly understand those last few words, and the sudden change in Helen's body language. I look over at Bella, muzzle-to-muzzle, and see that she caught it, too. And is starting to get all watery-eyed on me again. But this time the corners of her mouth are curling up instead of down.

So, I guess I'm gonna lose my very best girlfriend, after all. But I'll gain a sister in the process. A very precious sister. And that's a bargain I will gladly take any day. Every day for the rest of my life.

Acknowledgments

This book was not so much written as simply transcribed. If portions of this story seem a bit chaotic, the reality of my household is on a whole other level. It is nothing to have ten or eleven dogs and two or three cats racing pell-mell through my house every Christmas. And you'd think there would be some disagreements—God knows we humans struggle to stay perfectly civil with each other for just a few days every year. But most of the time the pets don't seem to ever notice. As long as breakfast is served in a timely manner and the doggie door to the backyard is left unlocked, they are perfectly happy and carefree little critters.

But the two years or so since I first published Private Eyes has been hard on our family, pet-wise. First Moose left us, then Fat Tony, and then in a very short period Dirk and Spot, two cats you would swear were identical twins. Still left to love are Minnie the Great Pyrenees mutt (who famously survived distemper as a puppy), Ellie the Pembroke Corgi, and dear little Patton, a rescue Australian Terrier who lost one eye when he was abandoned to fend for himself in a backyard for over a month. Actually, all three are rescues of a sort, even Ellie, who was so sick as a puppy they never bothered to dock her tail. And I will never again face life without a Corgi in it, stirring up as much trouble as those tiny little legs can manage. God sure packed a lot of dog into a tiny little package.

Once again, this book would be unfit for human, canine or even feline consumption but for the love and attention it received from my amazing editor, Kara Vaught. Her mastery of the English language is second to none, and this book is an excellent testament to that, Moose's creative mangling of that language notwithstanding.

The cover design comes from Cathy Helms at Avalon Graphics, whom I would highly recommend. Not only does she create what I think are fantastic covers with great eyeball appeal, she is also amazingly easy to work with. I gave her some general ideas, expecting to have to go through many, many iterations before she finally got it right, but to my surprise she hit it out of the ball park right off the bat. If you ever want your book judged in a positive way by its cover, call Ms. Helms.

As always, my everlasting thanks to Elizabeth, my greatest cheerleader, my inspiration, my best friend forever, and the keeper of my heart.

And, last but certainly not least, thanks to my real inspiration for this book, a ten pound bundle of absolute Aussie terror named Moose. He may be gone but he will never be forgotten. And Heaven will never be the same.

About the Author

Rene Fomby practices criminal defense and civil litigation across the state of Texas. A dedicated member of the State Bar's Pro Bono College, Rene takes on the nail-biting cases that most other lawyers turn away. And his life is ever richer for that.

More importantly, Rene is a winemaker, sailor, private pilot, helicopter dad and loving husband, and is currently owned by three very feisty dogs and countless adorable grand dogs and cats. And now, one brand-new human grandpuppy. (Who doesn't mind all the barking one tiny little bit!)

Other books by Rene Fomby

Private Eyes

Resumed Innocent (Sam Tulley Book 1)
The Chi Rho Conspiracy (Sam Tulley Book 2)
New Rome Rising (Sam Tulley Book 3)

The Game of War

Ready for the Next Chapter?

Please enjoy a sneak preview of the forthcoming new chapter in little Moose's life, With Her Majesty's Secret Corgis. Moose and Bella are living on a barge on the east side of London, and slowly adjusting to all the funny accents surrounding them, when a summons arrives from Barkingham Palace...

WITH HER MAJESTY'S SECRET CORGIS

rene fomby

London

S he glided effortlessly down the empty hall, nose held high in the air, her quick steps clattering noisily against the cold stone walls of the palace. With the Queen off at Windsor for the week, much of the palace staff had taken advantage of her absence to go on holiday themselves, leaving the castle desperately undermanned. And quite vulnerable, in her opinion.

But Ginger would have none of that. With the Queen away, that only meant the opportunity for mischief was doubled, making her job as head of the Secret Service even more difficult. If only she could teach her underlings to be as fastidious about their duties. But the youngsters they were hiring these days—bah!—no work ethic whatsoever. Just show up, put in the hours, then off to play. Well, nothing she could do about that. Except set an example, she supposed. Show them every single day what it would take to make top dog around here.

She waddled into the next hall, and the cluster of servants standing huddled together near the doorway trading gossip took one look at her trademark russet mane and quickly found something better to do. She made note of their names for her report at the end of the day. With the Queen away, the mice will play. Well, she'd certainly see about that!

A noise from close behind startled her, and she spun around quickly to see who was following her, but before she could make the turn completely she was swallowed up whole dog in a large and furry black sack. And then everything else went black.

But not before she got a whiff of a familiar old scent.

Beets.